1

The Music Box

BEKEZELA BROSCIUS

ISBN-10: 1986738841
ISBN-13: 978-1986738842

To my mother, Lerato Nare, who has been very supportive.
Thank you for being a wonderful mother and grandmother.

Chapter 1

I plopped on my chair, wishing I could vanish. Doreen sat right behind me. Last year she harassed me daily. Since every other desk in our classroom was taken, I stayed in my seat.

"I'm planning a class trip to either Victoria Falls or Matopos. Pair up and come up with ideas for fundraising for the trip," Mrs. Moya, our new teacher, said several minutes later. "I'll stick a sheet of paper on the classroom door. When you list your ideas, you don't have to reveal your names. But for now, write compositions about your vacation."

I almost leaped from my seat and smiled at the thought of going to either place. My classmates started chatting among themselves. Everyone seemed thrilled about the idea. But Mrs. Moya banged on her table with her ruler and everyone hushed. I imagined taking pictures of the great waterfall in Vic Falls or climbing the awesome granite hills in Matopos. Both places seemed far away from Phezulu, my hometown in southwestern Zimbabwe.

Maybe if I could come up with a fantastic idea for fundraising and help make the trip a success, my classmates would start treating me better.

While I was writing about the time I spent with Grandma, a girl who was barefoot and wearing a yellow floral dress with a huge green patch on it shuffled into the classroom. Doreen and her friends giggled, but the girl just smiled as if she didn't care at all what anyone thought of her. If I was the girl, this year I'd have tried to ignore them too. But last year, I'd have burst into tears and wished I could shrink so no one could see me. Doreen seemed to behave worse when I showed her I was hurting.

I smiled at the new girl in class and motioned her over. She pulled up a chair and sat down next to me. We would be sharing a desk that day.

As soon as Mrs. Moya noticed the girl, she stopped. "You must be Thabisa. Why are you so late and where's your uniform, young lady?"

"I'm sorry, ma'am," Thabisa said. "I had to help my mother sell sweets this morning." She bowed her head. "I don't have a uniform."

"You better have a uniform tomorrow. Otherwise, there'll be trouble. And there's no excuse for arriving late. Do you understand?" Mrs. Moya's voice rose with every word she spoke. "Write a composition about your vacation."

"Yes, ma'am," Thabisa said.

I drew a deep breath and looked at Thabisa. I

wished Mrs. Moya had been nice to her. After all, it was only the first day of school.

"Can I borrow a pen?" Thabisa whispered to me.

I gave her the pen in my hand. "Take this one. I have more. My name is Busi," I whispered back.

I was so nervous that my hand shook slightly as I dug into my backpack. I cared what Thabisa thought of me. I didn't want her to end up joining our classmates in singling me out.

After we all finished our compositions, we turned them in. We grew quiet as Mrs. Moya handed out papers with several word problems. Like the rest of the school, our classroom was like a prison with its boxlike shape and dull brown walls and all the desks close together. From where I was sitting, I could see a corner of the fence that surrounded the schoolyard, even though my seat wasn't next to the window. Giant gum trees grew along the school fence. The day was bright and the sky didn't have any clouds. I couldn't have asked for better weather for the first day of the term.

Before I finished the eighth question, Mrs. Moya collected our papers and slipped them in a folder. My hands trembled as I worried about getting a low score. Mrs. Moya would definitely scold me if I failed. Although I wasn't an 'A' student, I usually did much better than Doreen.

After my classes were over, I left Phezulu Primary and shuffled down the tarred road, which was lined by bare Jacaranda trees. I couldn't wait for their flowers to bloom. The purple blossoms always brought a smile to my face. Right now, the trees looked like giant statues grouped together with their arms raised. I wanted to lift my own arms up and sing and forget any worries. I shut my eyes briefly and breathed in the smell of the earth and relaxed my shoulders. The ground was still damp since it had rained a few days ago.

Everywhere I looked, kids from my school were walking down the paved street toward their homes. Boys were wearing khaki shorts and shirts, and navy blue ties, and girls were dressed in navy blue uniforms. My spirits sank when I realized that I was the only one walking alone. I constantly looked over my shoulder to make sure Doreen and her friend Ntando weren't following me. This year I wanted to avoid trouble whenever possible.

"Busi!" Thabisa called out. My heart skipped a beat as I spun around. "I heard someone talking about a school trip. Where are we going?" Thabisa was gentle and sweet, her tone of voice so different from the other kids' in class.

"Vic Falls or Matopos." I grinned and loosened my grip on my backpack. I often wished I could leave Zimbabwe and join my mother in Texas, U.S.A. But I also loved the thought of going on a school trip.

Thabisa's eyes lit up. "I've heard about the nice

rocks in Matopos. It's so great that I might finally see the place. Victoria Falls is just awesome too, of course. We're so lucky!"

"I also haven't been to either place. Should be lots of fun."

"Yeah, I'm sure we'll see and learn a lot. I'll definitely take notes."

"And lots of pictures, too." I slowed down and waved my hands as I spoke. "Would you like to be my partner? We could try to come up with a great idea for raising money."

"Do you have any ideas?"

I shook my head. "Not yet. But we could come up with something unique and brilliant so Mrs. Moya gives us a thumbs up." I chuckled.

"I'll help you think of something fun," Thabisa said.

"Great," I said. Now my whole body was relaxed and I felt totally comfortable with a peer for the first time in months. "I'm sorry Mrs. Moya kind of yelled at you. All the teachers at Phezulu Primary are really strict. I think the headmistress has some difficult rules for everyone to follow."

"I'm used to strict teachers, but anyway, I didn't expect all that on my first day of school."

I frowned. "Unfortunately, Mrs. Moya is the toughest of them all."

As we continued strolling along the road, we passed vendors seated on the pavement selling mangoes, bananas, papaya, and biscuits. I breathed in the scent of fruits and sweets and smiled. We greeted a woman selling apples while carrying a baby on her back. Now that I had left the school grounds and I was with Thabisa, my spirits were uplifted.

An elderly woman in a floral headdress knelt down on the pavement and slid a basket with oranges from her head, her dress sweeping the ground. A man played a drum to attract passersby to his wooden animal carvings and children surrounded him clapping their hands. I stopped walking and started tapping my feet and smiling. Thabisa had already joined the kids who were clapping and she started swinging her hips.

"Hey, you!" Doreen said from behind me and I turned around. Ntando stood next to Doreen smirking. My smile faded.

I drew a deep breath. What did Doreen want now?

"Anyway, I hope you don't go on the trip. You're so ugly, you'll scare all the animals away." Doreen poked at my temple. I tried not to wince. I was furious, but I tried not to show it.

I remained silent, pulled at Thabisa's hand, and continued walking as if Doreen hadn't treated me in a mean way or made nasty remarks.

"We don't want to go anywhere with you. We don't want you at this school," Doreen yelled after me. "You think you're so much better than everyone else. I wish my mother was also in America so I'd be rich like you."

My heart hammered and my stomach rumbled even though I'd brought lunch with me that day. I sighed when Doreen and Ntando didn't follow me.

"She was so mean to you," Thabisa said. "I can't believe she actually laid a finger on you. The things she said are so cruel. I'm sorry."

"I'll be okay." I smiled trying to hide my anger. "That's Doreen and Ntando. I'll try ignoring them even though the way they treat me hurts," I said as we continued walking.

The term was off to a bad start, but I knew why Doreen hated me so much.

In fourth grade, we had a teacher who often compared me to Doreen.

"Why aren't you well behaved like Busi?" the teacher would say to her. Then she'd add, "You should all follow Busi's example. She's polite and listens to me."

At lunch break, Doreen had followed me to the bench on which I sat all alone.

She pinched my nose. "You're so polite! Let me hear you say please, thank you, or I'm sorry."

"Leave me alone." I fought back tears and tried to push her away. If I were a first grader, I'd have reported her behavior to the teacher. But then I was almost nine years old.

When our classmates crowded around us to

watch, Doreen raised her voice. "Busi's the teacher's pet. Why should we copy her? She just wants to cause trouble for all of us." A few girls nodded, their eyes opened wide. Some trembled as they stared at Doreen, who was turning them against me.

Now that I was in sixth grade, I wished I knew how to stop the harassment.

"I'm home," Thabisa said, bringing me back to the present.

I stared at the bright brick house with a new roof and gasped. Despite the wilted red roses growing in the small yard, the house seemed nicer than mine, which had dull brick walls. How could someone with such a beautiful house not afford a school uniform?

"I only live a block away," I said. "See you tomorrow."

"I'm so glad I sat next to you. Bye."

I nodded and smiled. I hurried home feeling as if I were a fully inflated balloon, bobbing in the air. But I thought about my composition and remembered I'd forgotten to write my name on it. I inhaled deeply. What if Mrs. Moya punished me?

Grandma sat outside, her cane leaning against her chair. The lawn in the yard was long and green since we watered it when the soil dried up. I grinned as yellow butterflies fluttered about the guava trees in the front yard. When I reached Grandma, she rushed to me and hugged me.

"Afternoon, Grandma." I plopped my backpack

on the ground.

"My grandchild. I am happy you are home. How was your first day?"

"Okay."

"I hope you made a new friend."

"I sat next to Thabisa in class. She's the new girl in school." The words poured out of my lips, my excitement obvious as I waved my hands.

"I am very happy. I knew you would make a friend. You'll enjoy school this year." Grandma tried to stand up and I gave her a hand.

"Mrs. Moya is planning a school trip," I told Grandma where we were planning to go, and about the fundraiser.

"That is very good. You need to see those places. You'll learn something new."

I held Grandma's hand as we shuffled into the house. I squeezed her palm gently. Her wrinkled hand felt warm and comforting around mine. Whenever I held her hand, a warm feeling spread throughout my body and I felt protected. As if her touch were magical, it wiped away my sorrows.

"Your whole face is full of life today," Grandma said in the kitchen and settled in a chair I had pulled back for her. "Usually, you're not happy on first days of school. What is happening?"

I pulled my chair close to Grandma's so I could put my arm over her chair. "Thabisa seems like such a sweet girl. You should have seen the way she looked at me. She's so..." My voice trailed off. I'd been ready to compare Thabisa with Doreen, but I didn't want to ruin the good mood. Instead, I talked about how Thabisa and I had paired up to come up with ideas for fundraising.

"Good. You're trying harder to make friends. I am happy."

I laid my head on Grandma's shoulder. "I think this will be a good year for us all," I said, hoping Grandma would note how determined I was to make a difference in my school life.

In my room, I picked up my music box, which lay on the nightstand. I held it to my chest, and let out a breath. Then I laid it back down and the instrumental version of the song "Forever Your Friend" rang out. My heart pounded to the rhythm of the song as I remembered the day Florence, my old neighborhood friend, gave me the music box. We were sitting on a bench in the park, our feet crunching the grass. Florence clutched a bag in her hand.

"I'm leaving for Johannesburg. My parents found jobs there," she said.

"You can't be serious."

Florence hugged the bag in her hand. "I'm so sorry. I'm leaving in a few days."

I rubbed my eyes. "I'll miss you."

"Me too. I'll write often."

"What's in your bag, Florence?"

She grinned. "Guess."

"You have a yummy cake in there, right."

Florence giggled. "Try again."

"Let me think." I rubbed my temple and chuckled. "You have a mouse."

"Okay, you can give up guessing." Florence pulled out her music box from her bag and handed it to me. "You can have it."

I gasped. The music box fit perfectly in both hands. "But you got it from your mother."

"Yes, and she got it from a friend. Now I'm passing it on to you."

"How can I accept something so precious to you?"

"Mother said it's a token of friendship," Florence said. "It's meant to be passed from friend to friend."

I smiled and my eyes filled with tears. "Thanks so much."

I sniffled as I recalled the day Florence and I parted. The last text message I'd sent to her had been unanswered. I ran my hands along the fake gold cover of the music box. I wished my friend had never left Phezulu and that Doreen would leave and never come back.

Chapter 2

The next day, I awoke half an hour later than usual. After breakfast, I ran to school where I sat next to Thabisa, who wore the same dress she did yesterday. As soon as Mrs. Moya walked into the classroom holding a folder, everyone stood and greeted her. Then I slouched in my seat.

"Straighten up, Busi." Mrs. Moya pointed at me with a large ruler. She turned to Thabisa and stared at her long and hard. "I told you not to come back without a uniform. Please leave the classroom." Mrs. Moya clasped the ruler with both hands.

"But, ma'am—"

"No student at Phezulu should be allowed to attend lessons without a uniform. I won't have it." Mrs. Moya emphasized each word she spoke.

Thabisa grabbed the plastic bag with her pens and walked out of the classroom, her head bent. No one dared make a sound. I twisted my lips and sighed. If I was Thabisa I'd have burst into tears. If she didn't return to school, I would miss her. I needed a friend at school every day.

Mrs. Moya gave us math problems to solve, and then she sat down and pulled yesterday's math assignments and compositions from her folder. While working on the problems, I studied her face to see how she reacted to the assignments. She read the compositions first and stacked the ones she'd read on her table. Because Mrs. Moya didn't smile or frown, I couldn't guess what she was thinking. An hour later, I still struggled with the twenty math questions.

"Vumani," Mrs. Moya called one of the boys in our class.

"Yes, ma'am." Vumani walked to the teacher's table.

"Good job," Mrs. Moya said, handing him his composition.

I shook as the teacher called more students and returned their compositions. I knew why she wasn't calling my name.

Finally, Mrs. Moya waved my composition. "This composition is good, but I'll have to fail it because whoever wrote it didn't write his or her name."

I bowed my head. "It's mine. Sorry, I forgot to write my name."

"Raise your hand before talking. I can't let you get away with not writing your name. You're lucky this was a practice composition and that it won't affect your grades," Mrs. Moya said, her eyes fixed on mine.

My heart raced while she graded the math papers next. We were all now reading Ndebele textbooks. Ndebele was my native language and the only subject I excelled in. I scrutinized Mrs. Moya, frowned, and shook my head. I wished she were reading Ndebele assignments instead.

When she finished grading, she called me to her table first. "You only got four out of ten questions right," she said. "You didn't even finish. Do you want to go back to fifth grade?"

"No, ma'am."

"I can't believe you'll be in grade seven next year."

My heart sank. How could so much go wrong in one day?

Mrs. Moya scolded ten more students including Doreen, who had only gotten two questions right. At least Doreen was in trouble too. Maybe if she continued to fail, she'd become less popular.

"One student got everything right. But she can't be with us today," Mrs. Moya said, drawing a breath.

Thabisa had to be the one who excelled. She seemed to have such a good heart that I found it hard to be jealous of her, but I did wish that she were in school.

"I noticed that a few of you have already listed your ideas for fundraising for the class trip," Mrs. Moya said half an hour later. "I can't wait to see what the rest of you come up with." She held the sheet with the list of ideas in her hand. "Doreen and Ntando want us to have a talent show and Kwanele and Bongi want us to bake cakes. All these are good ideas."

When I turned around to face Doreen, she smirked and shook a fist at me. I bowed my head. Why hadn't I thought of any ideas for raising money? How could Doreen beat me to it? I squeezed my fists.

After school, I slung my backpack over my shoulders and walked home alone. I took a shortcut and walked down the dirt path in the woodland near the school. I hummed a tuneless song. My lips turned down when I realized how lonely I was without Thabisa at school. She could have become my closest friend and I'd have someone my age I could trust since Florence left.

As sparrows twittered and fluttered from branch to branch of *Mopane* trees, the events of the day ran through my head. I didn't stop to admire the yellow-green flowers and butterfly-shaped leaves. School was intolerable as usual and Mrs. Moya was helping make my life worse by sending my potential friend home.

I wiped the sweat on my face with my hands and grinned when an idea on how to help Thabisa popped into my head. Would Grandma agree to it?

When I reached the gate, I spotted Grandma on a chair in the shade, her eyes shut. As I entered the yard, she opened her eyes and smiled. She had a headdress covering her head and a shawl draped over her shoulders. She wore layers of clothing even on the hottest days of the summer.

"Grandchild. How was school?" she said.

I smiled at her. I hugged her, my backpack still on my back. "Just okay."

"How can that be? You made a friend."

I dodged the question. "Grandma, can I ask you something?"

She leaned back in her seat. "Sounds serious. What is the problem?"

I cocked my head. "Thabisa was sent home because she doesn't have a uniform. Can I give her one of mine?"

"What will you do? You need extra uniforms."

"Please, Grandma. Some of them are too small."

She paused and the wrinkles on her cheeks became more visible. "When I was a child, I did not wear a school uniform. Most of us were poor so no one cared. I admire what you want to do. So my answer is 'yes'."

"Thanks!" I grinned and nearly jumped in excitement. "I'll take one to her right away so she doesn't miss another day of school."

Inside my wardrobe, I found three uniforms, two of which I still wore. I took the smallest one, folded it, and put it in a bag. What would I say to Thabisa? I didn't want her to think I felt sorry for her. I didn't want anyone's sympathy, so I doubted Thabisa wanted mine.

The phone rang and I rushed to answer it. It was

Mama. I cried out so loud that Grandma entered the room.

"Mama!" I leaped and tears of joy filled my eyes. Mama only called a few times a month to check on us.

"Busisiwe. How are you, my dear daughter?" Mama was one of the few people who called me by my full name.

My lips spread into a broad smile. "I'm okay, Mama. I miss you so much! It's great to hear your voice! How are you?"

"I miss you too. I'm doing very well. Listen. I sent you a CD collection with wordless songs you can play even when you're writing. It's a gift from your dad and me."

Dad was also in America and my parents were divorced. He remarried a year ago and I hadn't heard from him for months. Sometimes I thought he forgot about me. My heart fluttered at the thought of *Baba* buying me CDs.

My pulse throbbed as I was anxious to hear more about *Baba*. "How's he?" I wished I had both parents with me.

"He's fine. He loves you, you know," Mama said.

"He never calls." I let out a groan and switched the phone to my left ear. If he really loved me, he would show it more.

"He will, don't worry. He's a busy man. I only hear from him once in a while myself and every time he asks about you."

"I called him and he didn't call back." I frowned. Didn't *Baba* know how much I missed him? Would he ever leave America to visit me?

Mama paused. "He will. I'll call him and tell him to write to you."

"Anyway, I'll keep writing until I hear word from him. I can't give up."

"That's my girl," Mama said. "You always persevere. I'll make sure you hear back, I promise."

After we spoke for several minutes, I handed the phone to Grandma.

"Busi made a new friend," Grandma said and I smiled. Grandma liked to tell Mama about everything that happened in my life.

Afterwards, I hurried toward Thabisa's with the uniform. When I reached the house where Thabisa and her mother lived, I tapped on the door. A woman with broad shoulders, wearing trousers and a man's shirt, opened the door. Thabisa appeared before the woman could say a word.

"Hi, this is Mrs. Nala, the owner of the house," Thabisa said. "Come on in."

"Hello, you must be Thabisa's friend. You cannot sleep here, you know," the woman said, walking away before I could respond.

"I'll show you my room, Busi. My mother and I rent one room." Thabisa grinned.

The room in which Thabisa and her mother slept

could barely fit a double bed. I tried not to step on the clothes cluttering the floor. A small wardrobe, with open drawers and a broken mirror, was squeezed between the bed and the wall. I smelled wax from a bottle with a candle. When a mouse scurried across the floor, I tried not to shudder. My heart went out to Thabisa and my lips twisted as I wished my friend lived in a better place.

"Sorry, there are no chairs," Thabisa whispered. "I don't like sitting in the living room with Mrs. Nala. She's strange sometimes." She crouched on the floor next to her clothes. I sat beside her, trying to smile even though the condition of the room made my heart sink.

"I've something for you." I gave Thabisa the bag in my hands.

Thabisa opened the bag and pulled out the uniform. "You shouldn't do this! I can't take it."

I smiled and murmured, "It's just a gift."

Thabisa shook her head. "I can't accept it. I'm sorry."

"Please do take the uniform. It's too small for me, anyway."

"Are you sure? What will your mother say?"

"Grandma said it's okay. I live with her," I said. "Mama goes to school in America."

"Wow. You must miss her."

I nodded and sniffled. "I do. I last saw her two years ago."

"That must be hard. I couldn't imagine being away from my mother for that long. Why don't you live with your mama?"

"I will someday," I said. "I miss her so, but Grandma loves it here and I want to be with her. I wish I could be in two places at once."

I remembered when I arrived in Phezulu three years ago. Grandma had wanted to move away from the city and be in a small and quiet town, so my mother recommended Phezulu. At first, I was disappointed, thinking I'd have nothing to do in a small town, but I found out that Phezulu had a theatre. I went to watch a movie once in a while.

"Please say yes to the dress," I said when my mind returned to the present time.

"Thank you so much. Now I can go to school. You're a good friend."

"You're welcome. Come on. Try the uniform on," I said.

Thabisa tried on the navy blue uniform, but it almost reached her ankles.

"I can shorten it for you," I said, folding the hem with my hands. "I took sewing lessons from Grandma."

"Don't worry. My mother and I will fix it."

"No, I'll do it. Your mother is busy." I smiled. "You'll be back at school tomorrow, I promise."

"Why don't we work on the uniform together?"

"Sure," I said.

Thabisa turned around and pulled out a pair of scissors, pins, and black thread from a wardrobe drawer. With her help, I managed to remove extra material from the uniform. Then we took turns hemming the dress.

"I haven't thought of an idea for fundraising, have you?" I asked.

Thabisa shook her head. "I've been busy worrying about what I'd do if I couldn't go back to school. Thanks to you, I'll go back."

We worked quickly and after we finished altering the uniform, Thabisa tried it on and twirled.

I held her hands and we spun around chuckling. "You go, girl! See you at school tomorrow." I continued laughing and I hugged Thabisa.

When I returned home, I called Dad using my landline, and left him a message saying I missed him and wished he could visit. Hopefully, I'd hear back from him soon and my life would take a turn for the better.

Chapter 3

As I walked outside with Thabisa during lunch break the next day, rain poured down and dripped from rooftops and trees onto the umbrella we shared. I sniffed the air, which smelled like mold. The rain had fallen hard suddenly, pelting the walls. Thunder roared, making me shudder. We ran into an empty first grade classroom with the alphabet written on the board and sat at a desk for two. I opened my bag and pulled out my lunchbox.

"I didn't bring any lunch." Thabisa's face fell. "It's raining too hard for me to go home."

"Have some of my sandwich. I'm happy to share." I opened my lunchbox and gave Thabisa half of my chicken sandwich.

"Thank you," Thabisa said. She took a bite of the sandwich. "This is better than having maize porridge for lunch every day."

"Let's think of ways to raise money. I don't want to ask my mother for it," I said.

"Maybe we could sell sweets. Mama sells sweets to raise money for groceries."

"Hmm. How about having a play? Some people will pay to watch a school play," I said, wiping crumbs from my mouth.

"That's a better idea, but who would be in it?"

"Our classmates. I'll list the idea," I said. "Everyone could try out for different roles."

"What if we perform *Cinderella*? It's one of my favorite stories."

"I love that story, too!" I said. "We could both have big roles. I've often dreamt of acting."

"You mean like a movie star?"

I nodded. "Let's jot the idea down now. We don't have to write down our names."

"Sounds great!"

"Would you like to come to my house on Saturday?" I asked Thabisa. "We could play pop and South African songs."

"I'd really like that."

That weekend, Thabisa arrived wearing a pink skirt, a white blouse covered with stains, and her school shoes. As I hugged her, I secretly wished I could give her half of my clothes to replace the worn out ones. We went straight to the sitting room where the music was playing.

Thabisa opened various CD cases. "I see you love music as much as I do."

"We seem to have a lot in common. Do you also like to dance?"

Thabisa twirled and I laughed. I admired the way she felt at ease.

In the kitchen, we helped Grandma boil and salt corn, groundnuts, and round nuts in the same pot to make *inkobe*. Afterwards, we carried the food from the kitchen to the sitting room to eat it. Grandma joined us and sat on the sofa next to Thabisa.

"The food tastes better than chips with vinegar, Grandma, thank you," Thabisa said.

Grandma smiled. "There is nothing as good as a traditional dish. I am glad you are enjoying it."

"We'll suggest our class perform *Cinderella* to raise money for the trip," I said.

"Very good! You children need to go and see the world. It's about time," Grandma said.

I grinned. "Thanks, Grandma. I wish you could join us."

"You should spend more time with children your age. You are growing up," Grandma said. "I will be there to see your play if my legs still work."

Now that I had Grandma's blessings, I could celebrate. Nothing could go wrong unless Doreen and Ntando tried to ruin my plan.

When Grandma was about to stand up, I tried to give her a hand.

"I can get up by myself. What do you think I do when you're at school?" Grandma waved her hands, smiling. She shuffled to her bedroom.

Thabisa and I washed the dishes. Afterwards, I headed to my bedroom with Thabisa where I showed her the music box.

"It's real pretty. You got it from your mother?" Thabisa said.

I shook my head. "It's from my friend Florence. She left Phezulu for Johannesburg before school opened."

"Can I touch it?"

"Sure."

Thabisa opened the music box. Her eyes opened wide as she ran a finger along the velvet inside of the box. "Is it made of gold?" She touched the yellow cover.

"It's not real gold."

The song "Forever your Friend" played. "I had a good friend once when I lived in the rural areas. We would gather firewood together and play ball. Our friendship ended when she moved to the city and I've only seen her a few times since. I really miss her." Thabisa handed the music box back to me.

"I know how you must have felt after she left. I felt like nothing would ever be the same without Florence. And I've lost touch with her already." My lips quivered. I wished Florence were with me now. She would have liked Thabisa too. She'd known that I was a big music lover.

I clutched the music box in my hands and sniffled as I thought about Florence. The music box was a perfect gift for me, one I'd cherish forever. Every time I listened to it, memories of the times I spent with Florence flooded my mind.

Last August, Florence and I had boarded a bus to the Historical Museum in Bulawayo without any adults and spent part of the day reading about the Ndebele people's movement from South Africa. After I returned to school, I wrote a composition about my visit.

"You're so stupid that no amount of time spent at the museum will help your grade!" Doreen had yelled in my ear during lunch break. "Obviously, your mother spoils you by giving you money to go there."

"That's not true," I said, stuttering.

"Busi," Thabisa said, and I stopped thinking about the past. "I wish I had music to listen to. We don't own a radio and I would never ask to listen to Mrs. Nala's. She's bitter."

"Why is she bitter?"

"My mother thinks it's because she doesn't have any children. She's not young anymore."

"Feel free to borrow my iPod."

"No, I can't."

"Come on," I said. "You love music as much as I do."

"Okay, thank you," Thabisa said. "I'll return it soon, I promise."

I waved a hand. "Keep it for as long as you want. I have the music box to listen to. I could listen to 'Forever your Friend' all day long." I smiled. Thabisa and I were quickly becoming good friends! I vowed not to let anyone try to bring us down.

Chapter 4

"To raise money for the school trip we'll perform *Cinderella*," Mrs. Moya announced in class the next afternoon.

Doreen raised her hand. "Why can't we have a talent show?" she asked.

"I like the idea of a *Cinderella* play much better."

"Can I be Cinderella?" Doreen asked.

"Doreen, I'll choose the cast for the play," Mrs. Moya said. "Everyone will have a part. Let's get back to work."

I grinned. Mrs. Moya had chosen my idea. I didn't comment, afraid my classmates would guess I'd thought of *Cinderella*. I imagined I was the fairy godmother and I was waving a magic wand to make Cinderella's dreams come true.

Before the end of the lessons, Mrs. Moya brought up the play again. "The play will be held in March before schools close. It'll take place on the school grounds," she said. "We'll have three rehearsals. I'll give you the dates for the rehearsals soon, but I expect you to start practicing tomorrow after the auditions."

"I'm going to start practicing Cinderella's lines. I'm sure I'll play her," Doreen said to Ntando after school.

"That's a good idea. I'll probably be the fairy godmother," Ntando said.

I folded my arms and stared at the two girls. How could they think they could play the best roles? That would allow them to continue trying to ruin my life. I cringed at the thought of Doreen playing Cinderella.

"What are you looking at?" Doreen said. "You should mind your own business." She picked up a book that lay on a desk next to hers and flung it at me.

I tried to duck, but the book landed on my head and I tried not to wince. Thabisa took my hand and squeezed it gently.

"You and Thabisa won't play Cinderella, so don't get your hopes up," Doreen said.

Ntando slapped hands with Doreen. "Let's go practice our lines. Obviously, we'll have big roles." She and Doreen laughed and they marched out of the room.

I turned my gaze to Thabisa, shaking my head.

Without commenting, Thabisa shrugged her shoulders. She was so gentle. What if Doreen and Ntando started picking on her too?

I couldn't wait for the school term to be over.

"Grandma, can Thabisa and her mother have supper with us?" I asked when I arrived home. I knew that

Grandma longed for an adult's company, so my idea of inviting Thabisa's mother, too, was perfect.

"Yes, I am happy you thought of that."

"Thanks, Grandma." I touched Grandma's shoulder and smiled. "I'll do most of the cooking."

Already I imagined Thabisa was Cinderella and I was the fairy godmother. I imagined Thabisa being transformed from a girl who wore ragged clothes to a princess wearing diamond rings and silky gowns.

Later Grandma and I fried chicken and cooked rice. Soon the kitchen smelled of garlic.

Thabisa arrived wearing a polka dot red dress with a wide hem, a bag in hand. Her mother had studs in her ears and curled hair. I thought Thabisa's mother was more dressed up than Thabisa whose shabby appearance suited a Cinderella character. I rushed to Thabisa and hugged her.

"I am glad you could make it," Grandma said. She shook Thabisa's mother's hands.

"Thank you for having us. I'm MaSibanda," Thabisa's mother said.

"This is for you, Grandma." Thabisa curtsied and gave a bag to Grandma.

Grandma opened the bag. "I love dried spinach. How did you know?"

Thabisa smiled. "We guessed. I hope you like it, too, Busi."

I nodded. The last thing I wanted was to admit to her that I hated dried vegetables.

Thabisa and her mother sat at the table while I helped Grandma dish the steaming hot food. As soon as we sat down and let the food cool, I devoured it. Several hours had passed since I had lunch, but Thabisa finished first. She said she was full when I offered her more.

"Busi said you will perform *Cinderella*," Grandma said. "I remember acting when I was a child. I was good."

I looked up from my plate and gazed at Thabisa. "We can't wait. I wonder who'll be Cinderella. Doreen really wants the role."

Thabisa clasped her hands over the table. "I can't wait to find out who I'll play. I hope I'm the fairy godmother."

"I want that part too," I said. "It's funny how we think alike."

"Thabisa is very excited about the play. That's all she's been talking about," MaSibanda said.

Grandma poured herself water from a jug. "Busi has been talking a lot about it too. I have never read *Cinderella*. But I am sure you will enjoy yourselves."

"I wonder who'll be the prince," I said. "I don't think any of the boys in class want to be a prince."

"We'll find out who'll be playing who soon," Thabisa said.

"So, where are you from originally, MaSibanda? Busi told me Thabisa went to your homeland last holiday," Grandma said.

"Khezi," MaSibanda said.

"My grandmother was from Khezi, so we are family. She was also a Sibanda." Grandma smiled.

"I'm so happy I met you. You are family," MaSibanda said.

"Hey, we are cousins," I said to Thabisa and grinned.

Thabisa and her mother would probably be visiting often. Grandma considered them relatives because they were from her homeland. She seemed to like and trust them.

"In Khezi we have a lovely homestead with several huts for the many relatives who visit," MaSibanda said. "Thabisa seems to love it even though there's no electricity and we cook over fires."

"My granddaughter should get together with Thabisa in Khezi one of these days," Grandma said.

I turned my gaze to Grandma and smiled.

I nudged Thabisa after dinner. "Let's go practice *Cinderella* for fun."

In my bedroom, I pulled a tattered dress and a long frilly white gown from my wardrobe.

"Pretend we're both Cinderella. Why don't you try this dress on?" I laid the gown on Thabisa's shoulder.

"I'll wear the ripped one. This one looks big."

"Okay," I said. "I have an apron to go with the ripped dress."

We giggled as we changed into our costumes.

I twirled. "Oh, Prince, dance with me. Am I not the luckiest girl in the world?" I said in a lilting voice.

"Nice," Thabisa said. "Cinderella would talk to the prince like that."

"Your turn."

"I'll stay home all day doing nothing but dream about the ball. Oh, I wish I were there now." Thabisa pretended she was Cinderella scrubbing the floor.

We laughed so loud that Grandma checked on us to find out what we were doing. Afterwards, I couldn't help talking about Doreen and how she could ruin the whole play.

"But she doesn't know we thought of the idea," Thabisa said, pulling the apron off.

"If Doreen isn't chosen to be Cinderella and one of us is, she'll make us miserable."

"Don't worry about her."

"I can't help it. Anyway, I'm not fit to be Cinderella. My nose is crooked." I caught my reflection in the wardrobe mirror and looked away.

"Don't say such things. You're very pretty."

"Thanks. You really think so?"

I thought my forehead was too wide. What I liked about my appearance was my long and slim fingers. My fingernails grew fast, but I kept them short. Although I helped Grandma around the house, my hands were smooth as if I never washed clothes or dishes. She wanted us to do the housework ourselves and didn't like having a maid. Even though her back bothered her, she still found time to keep the house neat.

Thabisa and her mother stayed until the moon was out.

"We really should get going," MaSibanda finally said. "It's very late."

"Do you want to stay overnight?" I said to Thabisa.

"We have a spare bedroom," Grandma said, "and extra towels."

"No, thank you. We live close by. Maybe Thabisa will stay over another night," MaSibanda said and stood up. "We'll help you wash up then get going."

I cleaned the table and swept the floor while Thabisa and her mother did the dishes. The day had gone fast after they arrived. I wished they could stay forever. And when I remembered that tomorrow I'd be trying out for the role of Cinderella, my hands shook.

Chapter 5

Mrs. Moya waved a copy of the *Cinderella* play. "Everyone should audition. You can choose who you want to play and read a few lines for that character. You can audition for up to two roles. I'll decide who plays the different roles," she said. "Let's get started."

More than half of the girls in my class wanted to play Cinderella. When Doreen dashed to the front of the class to be the first one to audition, I decided to play Cinderella instead of the fairy godmother. Since Thabisa also wanted to play the fairy godmother, I would have to compete with her for the role. Wasn't it better to compete with Doreen instead? When I stood in line to audition, thinking things over, Doreen scowled at me. I didn't say anything to her.

Doreen read a line from the play with confidence. " 'I wish I could go to the ball, but I don't have any nice clothes. Why would the prince choose to dance with me?' " Her voice sounded hoarse as if she had a bad cold. I didn't think Doreen sounded good at all. As if she wanted our classmates' approval, she faked a smile and tried to make eye contact with each one of them.

"Thank you, Doreen," Mrs. Moya said before

Doreen could continue. Doreen shuffled to her seat, muttering words to herself, her head bent down.

My heart pounded when it was my turn to read Cinderella's lines. Would I be able to perform better than Doreen? I shook as I stood reciting the same lines as Doreen. When I looked up, my classmates' eyes were fixed on me, and Thabisa was the only one who was smiling at me, her eyes bright. I read louder than I had intended to. I gazed at Thabisa and pretended that no one else was in the room. My shoulders relaxed and my heart stopped beating fast.

" 'Thank you, Fairy Godmother. Now that I have a lovely dress and a carriage, I can go to the ball. I will leave the ball before midnight.' " I read my lines clearly. I sounded as if I were belting a song.

Since I read more lines than Doreen before Mrs. Moya interrupted me, I hoped the teacher liked the way I performed.

Thabisa stood in front of the class to audition to play the fairy godmother. " 'I can make all your wishes come true, Cinderella.' " She cleared her throat before she continued. Although Thabisa stuttered a few times, I thought she had performed well. I clapped my hands after Thabisa read her lines, but some of my classmates folded their arms.

When Ntando stood in front of the class to recite the fairy godmother's lines, I hoped she'd stumble. Ntando grinned throughout her audition. I believed that Thabisa would play the fairy godmother, but I wasn't optimistic about playing Cinderella. Doreen also auditioned for the role of Cinderella's stepmother.

"I've decided the cast for the play," Mrs. Moya said after the auditions. "Busi will play Cinderella. She performed better than anyone else."

"Congratulations, Busi." Thabisa patted my shoulder.

I grinned, glad that she didn't resent me for playing Cinderella.

My plan to beat Doreen in everything was working well. Not only had I come up with an idea for fundraising our teacher approved, but I'd also get to play a role that would put me in the spotlight. Everyone would get to know me as the girl who played a memorable role in the school play, the girl whose idea made the school trip possible. None of my classmates commented about my role as Cinderella. A few shook their heads, but most of them remained serious, obviously not impressed by the teacher's decision.

Please let Thabisa be the fairy godmother. I held my breath as I waited for the teacher to announce more roles. Thabisa kept her head up and smiled even though the teacher hadn't given her a role. I grinned at Thabisa, admiring her for not showing any sign of nervousness.

"Doreen, you'll play Cinderella's stepmother,"

Mrs. Moya said.

Doreen looked at me and smirked. "Yes."

My heart sank. I inclined my head. Why did Doreen have to play a major role? Just when things seemed to be going my way, Doreen got a role that would allow her to put me down. The last thing I wanted was for the audience to cheer for her and not me. After all, she was somewhat a leader in school.

"Kwanele will play the fairy godmother," Mrs. Moya said.

My face fell. Why didn't the teacher choose Thabisa to play the fairy godmother? She'd given a good performance. Thabisa stopped smiling. She looked at me and shrugged. Ntando grumbled because she didn't get the role of fairy godmother. Vumani would play the prince and two girls who hardly spoke to me would play Cinderella's stepsisters.

Mrs. Moya paced the room. "We'll need costumes. Also, when the prince marries Cinderella at the end of the play, he could give her something other than a ring. Any ideas?"

Kwanele said, "What about a purse? I think a silver purse will go well with Cinderella's gown."

"Do you have the purse?" Mrs. Moya asked.

"No, ma'am."

"We can't afford to spend money on props," Mrs. Moya said.

"Maybe the prince could give Cinderella flowers,"

Vumani said.

"That's a good idea," Mrs. Moya said. "But I was thinking of something that lasts a while. Flowers dry up easily."

I raised my hand. "I have a music box that the prince could give to Cinderella. I also have clothes that others could wear for the play."

My classmates groaned. My face felt as if it was burning and I clenched my hands tightly, ready to explode. But I decided that Mrs. Moya would be disappointed or angry with me if I withdrew the offer. I faked a smile and held my head up anyway even though my head was now aching from tension.

"A music box would be a perfect gift for Cinderella. Thank you, Busi," Mrs. Moya said and turned to the class. "I want you to read the play. There are three copies available in the library and we can't afford to order more, so you'll have to share."

Kwanele raised her hand. "How are we going to get to Matopos or Victoria Falls?"

"That's a good question," Mrs. Moya said. "I was going to talk about that anyway. We'll take a bus from here to Bulawayo and travel from there to our destination. We should get a discount since we are traveling as a group. Some of you will be responsible for selling tickets for admission to the play."

After the bell rang for lunch break, I felt a nudge on my shoulder as Thabisa and I were walking out the door. I turned around and faced Doreen.

"What do you want?"

Doreen put her hands on her hips. She bumped my shoulder with her broader one. "I'm not wearing any of your filthy clothes. I know you think you can save the day just because you're rich. I'll wear my uniform if I have to."

"Suit yourself," I said, looking Doreen straight in the eyes.

"You think you can offer this and that to make yourself look good. No one likes you because you like to show off. Don't think you're still Miss High and Mighty just because you're going to be Cinderella," she said. "I'm the stepmother, remember? I won't be acting when I put you down."

"Hey, let's keep going," Thabisa said to me.

I turned to Doreen. "I was only trying to help." My lips shook. I immediately regretted my comments. After all, Doreen *was* trying hard to make me upset. I had long realized it was better to ignore her.

"Just go, okay, before I lose my temper and squash your small brains." Doreen strutted away, and Ntando, who'd just appeared from the classroom, smirked. There was more to come. Doreen and Ntando wouldn't stop until they brought me down.

"Don't mind them," Thabisa said. "Let's go to the library before all the *Cinderella* books are checked out."

We hurried to the library. A small classroom had

40

been converted into a library a few years ago. We searched the books lined on shelves against the wall. To my relief, one copy of *Cinderella* was available, so we checked it out. Afterwards, we had lunch in the shade.

"I'm sorry you didn't get the role of the fairy godmother. You performed well," I said, my mouth full.

"I *am* disappointed, but I'll be okay. I'm so happy you got the main role."

"I wish I didn't offer my music box, but it's too late to take back the offer. What if they damage it? It means a lot to me. I care about it as if it were a living thing if that makes sense."

Thabisa nodded. "I hear what you're saying. You were simply being generous."

I still couldn't believe Mrs. Moya had chosen my idea of performing *Cinderella*. She seemed to like me, but nothing I did so far was bringing me closer to being accepted by anyone else in our class besides Thabisa.

Chapter 6

When I returned home, I found Grandma sitting on the kitchen floor, muttering to herself. Chips from a broken plate lay scattered on the floor.

"What happened, Grandma?" I cried out and grasped her shoulders. "Are you hurt?"

She shook her head. "I slipped," she whispered, her speech slurred. "It just happened. I am not hurt." But something was very wrong. Grandma wasn't her normal self. No matter how hard I tried to lift her, I failed.

"I'm going to get MaSibanda, okay, Grandma?"

Grandma nodded, her head tilted to the side. Without wasting time, I ran all the way to the Nalas, sweat trickling down my face. When I reached their house, I banged on the door with my fists and opened it before someone answered. MaSibanda stood in the kitchen grinding nuts with a bottle.

"MaSibanda, please come quickly!" I shouted. "My grandma's on the kitchen floor and her voice sounds strange. I need help lifting her."

MaSibanda set the bottle aside. "I'll be there right away."

Mr. and Mrs. Nala entered the room. "We heard what you said," Mr. Nala said. Next to Mrs. Nala, he was like a sugar cane stalk, tall and thin. "We're coming with you."

When we reached my home, Grandma was now lying on the floor, her right hand shaking. She whispered my name, stuttering.

"I hear you, Grandma," I said through tears. "We're here to help. We'll take care of you."

"She's having a stroke," Mr. Nala said.

How serious was the stroke? Would Grandma be okay? My eyes flooded with tears and my lips trembled.

With MaSibanda and Mrs. Nala's help, Mr. Nala lifted Grandma up and sat her in a chair. "We've got to get her to the hospital," he said.

"I'll go and get the car," Mrs. Nala said. "An ambulance won't get here fast enough." She hurried out the door.

"I'll come with you," MaSibanda said.

"No, you stay with the children," Mr. Nala said. He held Grandma's hand and MaSibanda put her arm around her. I held Grandma's other hand, and she managed to shuffle outside.

"I'm coming with you," I said. I had to make sure Grandma was all right.

"Our car is a little too small for everyone," Mr. Nala said.

"I have to be with my grandma!" I cried.

MaSibanda nodded.

When Mrs. Nala returned, I sat in the backseat of

the Nalas' car with Grandma, who leaned on me and continued to whisper my name.

I wrapped my arms around Grandma. "You'll be okay, Grandma." There was a tremor in my voice and I knew I didn't sound confident.

The nearest hospital was thirty minutes away. Mrs. Nala drove away from Phezulu, heading toward Bulawayo, past the small houses shaped like matchboxes.

I stared out the window. Clouds parted and the sunlight spilled through the window, but tears trickled down my face. How could anything happen to Grandma? Last night she and I had talked for hours before bed and she'd appeared in good health. When I left for school, she'd smiled at me as she said goodbye. How could Grandma have a stroke in a short matter of hours?

Soon we left Phezulu, passed jagged hills, and farms with tall grasses, shrubs, and wildflowers. Goats were grazing on the vegetation. Today the scenery didn't cheer me up and it didn't match my mood. What would I do without Grandma?

Mr. Nala turned to face me. "Your grandma will be fine. I'm glad you came to us right away. The doctors will take good care of her."

Was he saying so because he didn't want me to be upset? I wanted to trust him, but it wasn't easy. I rubbed my eyes and squeezed Grandma's hand gently. Grandma had stopped talking. Her eyes were closed and her lips quivered, and she continued to rest her upper body on me. I didn't complain or shift. I wished I could do more.

When we arrived at the hospital, Mr. Nala rushed into the two-story brick building and returned with a wheelchair. He and Mrs. Nala helped Grandma out of the car. He wheeled Grandma into the hospital and Mrs. Nala and I hurried behind him. A doctor examined Grandma right away and the Nalas and I sat in the waiting room.

"She seems to be having a stroke. We'll tell you more after we admit her," the doctor said to us minutes later.

"Will she ever walk well again?" I said, my heart pulsing.

"As I said, we'll have more information after we examine her."

I cracked my knuckles as I waited to hear more from the doctors, feeling smothered in the narrow waiting room. The sunlight poured into the room, scorching my bare arms. A woman entered the room sobbing. She clung to a man who could have been her husband. Had she lost someone she loved? My eyes streamed with tears as I imagined Grandma lying helpless on the hospital bed. The Nalas were now talking low to each other, so I was left out. I wished I had a Ndebele novel to distract me, but I didn't see a single book or magazine. Finally, one of the doctors said I could see Grandma.

She lay in bed on an incline. Her cheeks sagged more than usual and her eyes had sunk into her face. Her parched lips curved into a crooked smile. I smiled back and sat in a chair next to her.

"How are you, Grandma?" She fought back tears. Grandma had aged a decade in a matter of hours.

"I will be fine, Busi. I hope I don't stay here a long time," Grandma said, her speech less slurred. "Who will look after you?"

"I'll be okay for a few days," I said. "I could invite Thabisa and her mother over so you won't worry."

"That is good. Tell them they are very welcome."

Although I liked the thought of staying with Thabisa, I was still worried that I wouldn't see Grandma again.

"I want to see your play, so don't give up on it," Grandma murmured.

I nodded. "I won't, Grandma. I'll be playing Cinderella." I tried to smile even though I was worried about Grandma.

"That is good. I promise I'll come home very soon. I am not going anywhere."

I tried to smile. "I hope you get better soon."

"What will you do while I am here?"

How could I have any fun while Grandma was in the hospital? "I'll play the music box with Thabisa. I'll think about you all the time and try not to worry."

When I asked the doctor how Grandma was doing, he told me she was a strong woman and he added that the stroke was mild. Was he being honest when he told me the stroke was mild? Mr. Nala had to return to his house, so I left with him and Mrs. Nala.

As Mr. Nala drove toward Phezulu, I looked out the open window trying not to worry about Grandma. The sky had darkened and the sun hid behind gum trees. The car screeched and the smell of exhaust fumes made me wrinkle my nose.

When we reached my house, Thabisa and her mother were waiting.

"How is Grandma?" Thabisa asked.

"The doctors said she'll be fine. She's a tough woman," I said. My eyes were now dry, but my head ached. I felt as if I hadn't slept for days. "Can you stay with me until Grandma is discharged from the hospital?" I asked Thabisa and MaSibanda.

"We'd love to," MaSibanda said.

"I'd love to spend time with you." Thabisa smiled.

"I'm sure Grandma will be happy. Thanks so much," I said.

After Thabisa and her mother left, I called Mama and left a message on her cell phone.

Mama returned the call fifteen minutes later. "I'm coming to Zimbabwe," she said.

"You're leaving Texas?" My heart thumped as I longed to see Mama.

"I have to see my mother. What did the doctors

say?"

"The doctors said she'll be fine. But I want to see you, too, Mama. It's been so long."

"How does she look?"

I rubbed an eye and sniffled. "She looks much older, but the doctors said the stroke is mild."

"You must be home alone, my poor daughter."

I explained that Thabisa and her mother would be staying with me and I also told Mama that Grandma trusted them.

"That's great. I'll be there within a few days. I love you."

"I love you too."

Everything was happening fast. Mama was coming after being away for years, but I wished the circumstances were different.

Chapter 7

When Thabisa and I were walking into the class-room the following day, our classmates whispered and pointed at us. I overheard someone saying, "Her grandmother," and drew a deep breath. The news about my grandmother's illness must have already spread throughout the neighborhood. I wished people would stop talking about Grandma behind my back. Why couldn't my classmates just come to me instead of counting on rumors? I bit my lip as I thought of them gossiping about Grandma.

Doreen walked toward my desk. What could she want now? I squeezed my knuckles with my palm.

"I'm sorry your Grandma is sick," Doreen said.

"Thank you," I said. Did Doreen really mean the words she'd said? She'd spoken with a straight face.

"That doesn't mean I want to be friends with you at all. I know that you thought of the play."

Since ignoring Doreen hadn't worked before, I was going to answer back. "What if I did?" I looked at her without flinching and tried not to show any emotion.

"You always think you're better than anyone else and that your ideas are superior. I'll prove you wrong."

I held my breath. "That's not true." My heart was hammering, but I hoped Doreen couldn't hear the sound.

"I'll destroy your dream."

"What do you mean?" I said in a calm voice.

Doreen grimaced. "You don't think I know what's on your mind? You offer a music box, clothes, the idea for a play, and you make sure you play Cinderella. Obviously, you want attention. You never offered stuff before." She wasn't as dumb as I had thought. I had to be on guard around her. She turned to Thabisa. "The only reason you stick with Busi is because you think she can give you nice things."

Thabisa eyes bulged. "Busi is my friend."

"Leave Thabisa out of this. We didn't do anything to you," I said.

"Stop showing off! No one needs your stuff," Doreen said.

I kept my shoulders straight and folded my arms, trying to appear unfazed by what Doreen had said. "I was only trying to help."

"You'll be lucky if you play Cinderella or if that play takes place at all."

I put my hands on my hips. "What do you mean?"

Doreen chuckled. "You don't get it, do you?" She turned and walked away. I hurried after her for more answers.

"Stop following me!" she shouted so loudly that I froze on the spot.

Should I tell Mrs. Moya that Doreen might try to ruin the play? Could I really tell the teacher without any evidence? I needed to talk to someone and try to figure out what Doreen was planning. Maybe Thabisa could help somehow. I had to come up with a plan to save the play I knew I'd love to act in. Playing Cinderella was my chance to be noticed and the majority of my classmates might end up liking me. Also, the play had to take place for us to go on a trip. Maybe I'd even be a hero.

Should I talk to Ntando when Doreen wasn't around to learn more about their plans? I thought Ntando was a follower, not a leader, so she was more likely to reveal more information. How could I get Doreen and Ntando away from each other? The two seemed inseparable. I had to approach Ntando when she was alone. I decided to confront her on her way home after she'd said goodbye to Doreen.

During lunch break, I told Thabisa my plan to ask Ntando how Doreen planned to ruin the play.

"I know where both of them live." I crumpled a green leaf. "Doreen's house is closer to the school, so we should follow them all the way to her house. Ntando walks the rest of the way home alone, so we could talk to her once she's by herself. If we keep our distance, they won't notice who we are or that we're following them."

"Good idea!" Thabisa said. "We can't let them spoil the play. When do you plan to do this?"

"Today. I won't waste any time."

"I care about the play too. I'm sure a lot of our classmates do, so they'd really be disappointed if it doesn't take place," Thabisa said. "You don't believe what Doreen said about me, do you?"

"Of course not. She thinks she rules the world."

After school, we were the first ones to leave the classroom. I thought Doreen would be suspicious if we left the classroom when she did. Thabisa and I hid behind Jacaranda trees near the school and waited for Doreen and Ntando to pass by.

"I hope they don't decide to take a different route. I really need to talk to Ntando now," I said.

"Don't worry," Thabisa said. "They'll show up."

But when several minutes passed with no sign of Doreen and Ntando, I began to crack my knuckles. Thabisa and I remained hidden behind the trees, which were several feet from the road. I ran my fingers along the scaly tree trunk. I took in a deep breath, then slowly let it out. Robins sang in the trees. I hoped they wouldn't attract Doreen and Ntando's attention.

Finally, Doreen and Ntando came into view and walked past the trees. When they were far enough not to recognize us easily, Thabisa and I crept out of our hiding place. Doreen and Ntando didn't look back. When Thabisa and I reached Doreen's house we slowed down and waited until Doreen said good-bye to Ntando. After Doreen entered her house, we followed Ntando until Doreen's house was out of sight. Then we ran up to Ntando.

"Ntando!" I called out.

"What? Were you following me?" she asked, clutching her backpack tight.

"I want to know how you're planning to ruin the play."

"What makes you think that? I don't have to answer to you anyway."

"I know you and Doreen are up to something. Say what it is."

"You're trying too hard to be a bully. Why wait until I'm all by myself when you've a friend with you?" Ntando folded her arms. "We're not planning to ruin the play. In fact, we want to go to Victoria Falls or Matopos. We just want you out of this school. We're trying to get rid of you, not the play."

"What did I do to you?" I asked. I definitely didn't feel as intimidated by Ntando as I did by Doreen.

"Don't act like you don't know why no one likes you. You're going down."

"I'm not sure why you hate me so much," I said. "I hope you're not hiding anything else."

Ntando turned away without saying another word.

"I don't know whether or not to believe her. About there not being anything else planned, I mean," I said. "Doreen did say before that the play won't take place."

"Don't worry. Mrs. Moya won't let them do anything to stop the play from taking place."

"Of course," I said, but I still had doubts.

That afternoon I boarded a bus with Thabisa and MaSibanda to visit Grandma at the hospital.

Grandma tried to smile when she saw us. "Hello," she said, her speech less slurred than before. She sat on the hospital bed, her legs covered with cream sheets, and she had matching pillows behind her back. She took my hand in her wrinkled one and smiled. "I miss being home with you."

"I miss you, too, Grandma." I smiled as I sat on a chair next to the bed. I was relieved that she seemed to be recovering well. "Mama called. She's coming to see you."

"All the way from America? What about her studies?" Grandma asked.

"You're much more important to all of us." I squeezed her hand. "She'll arrive in a few days. I can't wait to see her. Hopefully, you'll be discharged soon."

"I will. I am feeling much better. We'll even travel to new places."

I remembered how much more active Grandma had been a few years ago when we'd traveled to Botswana and South Africa by train together. When I traveled with Grandma, I had a friend I could always count on. Since she had a story about each area we visited, I was entertained. Now I realized that her companionship had helped me overcome my loneliness. Was being accepted by my schoolmates that important? Why did the way they treat me sometimes hurt so much? More than anything, I wanted Grandma to recover and live her normal life again.

Grandma turned to Thabisa and MaSibanda. "You are good to my granddaughter. Thank you."

"Would you like us to bring you anything?" MaSibanda asked.

Grandma shook her head. "I am fine. I just want to leave this hospital."

"I hope you'll be discharged soon," I said.

"Get well soon," Thabisa said.

When we stepped outside, the wind blew gently, and the sky was clear. The day was perfect for a stroll. As we passed yards with mulberry trees, I wished I could taste the juicy fruit and forget my worries. I sniffed the air. The scent of tar, mint, and dirt combined made me grin for the first time since leaving the hospital. When we returned home, Thabisa and I did homework, and MaSibanda headed to her room.

In the evening, Mama called again. "I'm leaving Texas. I'll arrive in Bulawayo in a couple of days, then take a taxi to Phezulu."

"I can't wait to see you, Mama."

"Me too, Busisiwe. I miss you so much."

That night I couldn't sleep, thinking about Mama's arrival. I also dreamed about Grandma. In the dream, I was on stage in a big theatre filled with my classmates and the neighborhood kids. Grandma sat in the front row cheering, but the children booed. I kept saying, "You can't hurt me," until Mrs. Moya entered the stage, and yelled, "Busi."

I shouted, "My name is Cinderella!"

I awoke when Thabisa shook me to let me know it was time to go to school.

Chapter 8

"I have good news for you," Mrs. Moya said to our class before she started teaching. "The play will be advertised in the local paper so more people can learn about it. Since not everyone reads the paper, I still expect you to spread the word any way you can. I finally have an exact date for the play. It will be held on the thirtieth of March."

I nodded as I listened to Mrs. Moya talk about how important it was to attract a large number of people and how the money would determine whether or not we went on a trip. I decided to brainstorm ideas for making the play known to more people. While Mrs. Moya taught, I pondered and came up with the idea of making posters and putting them on trees lining the streets, in the park, and other public places. During lunch break, I shared my idea with Thabisa and when we returned home, we decided to get started right away.

"We need to get papers big enough to make posters, we could even put a poster on the store door so everyone who walks in can see it, let's decide what to write," I said without pausing as I pulled a pen and paper from my backpack.

"Where can we get papers to make posters?"

Thabisa asked, sitting on the floor.

"I know. Mama always sends me things in cardboard boxes. Maybe we could stick large papers on flat cardboard boxes to make big posters, then tie the posters to trees. I think I've everything we need to do that. We could even ask our classmates to help, but not Doreen and Ntando."

"You always come up with clever solutions," Thabisa said. "Why don't we get started?"

When we reached my house, we went straight to my bedroom, and rummaged through drawers for papers. We slipped the papers in a bag. In the kitchen, we picked up a few boxes, which sat flattened next to a trashcan. I spread papers on the floor, found some glue, and stuck them on the cardboard. I didn't have any strings strong enough to use to tie the posters onto trees, so I decided to sew yarn on the edges of the cardboard posters, then tie the yarn around the trees.

I put tape in my backpack. "It's a good thing we had everything we needed." I sat on the bedroom floor and crossed my legs. "Do you really think we should try to get our classmates to help?"

"I don't see why not," Thabisa said. "If everyone puts a poster on his or her street, word will spread faster, and we won't have to go to each and every street in town."

"You have a point," I said. "We can start by putting posters on the Jacaranda trees on my street." I stood up, holding up a poster. "Let's get started."

Outside the air smelled fresh and the sunshine streamed in through the trees, warming my face. Thabisa and I spent time securing the posters to the Jacaranda tree trunks. A woman and a child in a donkey-driven cart filled with groceries looked at a poster. I grinned, hoping they would spread the news.

Then Thabisa and I went toward the Nala's with the remaining posters and put them on trees on the Nala's street.

The next day I went to school early.

"Would you like to help me put up posters to advertise the play?" I asked classmates who were already there.

Most of them didn't even pay attention to me and continued chattering amongst themselves. Only Kwanele looked up at me.

"I'll do it," she said and I sighed with relief.

"Great," I said.

Doreen and Ntando hadn't arrived yet, so at that moment I didn't have to worry about them giving me a hard time for coming up with yet another idea. At lunch break, while Thabisa and I were eating, Kwanele came to us.

"You come up with good ideas, Busi. I wish I could too." Kwanele settled next to us. "What can I do to help?"

I smiled. "Thanks, Kwanele. Could you put posters on your street? We were putting some on trees. If you like, you could even put them on street signs or your bus stop. We could make the posters and give them to you."

Kwanele waved her hand. "Don't worry about making the posters for me. I can make a few and write a note about the play. It shouldn't be hard."

"Sounds good," Thabisa said. "Now we have to worry about where everyone will sit on the day of the play."

We all chuckled. Maybe not all of the Phezulu students wanted to hurt me. Before leaving, Kwanele gave us each a high five. In the distance, I spotted Doreen and Ntando, but they didn't come to bother me and Thabisa. I was relieved they hadn't teased me for coming up with the idea of making posters.

In class, Mrs. Moya announced that there'd be a rehearsal the following week. My palms sweated since I hadn't started memorizing my lines. A few of my classmates gasped and started talking to each other. Mrs. Moya banged on the table with her ruler to silence everyone.

Soon after the last lesson ended, I looked up from my desk and found myself face-to-face with Kwanele.

Kwanele held out her hand. "May I borrow your book? I haven't had a chance to look at my lines."

"I haven't had a chance to look at mine either. Maybe we could study together sometime."

"Can I take a quick look at it right now?" She grinned.

"Sure." I dug the book out of my bag and handed it to her.

I expected her to stay nearby, instead, she headed outside. I called out to her, but she didn't turn around.

"Where do you think she's going with my book?" I asked Thabisa.

"Do you want us to go after her?"

We stood up and when we were outside, Kwanele was nowhere in sight. Doreen and Ntando sped past us. Doreen was waving my copy of the play. My mouth dropped open.

"Hey, where did you get that?" I asked. It dawned on me that Kwanele had used me to give the copy to Doreen and now I might never see my library book again. My shoulders drooped. How was I going to learn my lines? I doubted any of my classmates with copies of the play would be willing to lend me one. I trembled at the thought of not being able to recite my lines. Somehow, I had to come up with a plan to get my copy back. Maybe I could talk Kwanele into taking the book back from Doreen. If I approached Doreen directly, she could tear the library book to pieces.

While we were putting more posters in the neighborhood later that day, I told Thabisa my plan.

"Do you think Kwanele would agree to get the

book from Doreen?" Thabisa said, taping a poster on the store door.

"I hope so," I said. "Maybe wc could offer to give her something in return."

"Are you sure?"

I nodded. "I'll do anything to act in the play. It means a lot to me. It is my chance to be noticed and to prove I can act."

"Go with your plan then."

"I should have known that Kwanele was using me when she agreed to help with the posters. How could I have been so blind not to see it?" I said.

"That's because you're such a positive person. You don't think bad things about other people."

I smiled. "That describes you, not me."

The following day I confronted Kwanele when I met her on the way to school.

"Why did you give my book to Doreen?" I held my chin up and folded my arms.

"She made me do it. She said if I didn't she'd make me regret it." Kwanele bowed her head. "Can I go to school now?"

"Can you get my book back? You could just tell Doreen that you're borrowing it."

Kwanele shook her head. "I can't."

"Why not?"

"Because Doreen would make me pay for going behind her back."

"But the book is mine, not hers."

"Sorry, I can't help you." Kwanele stared ahead, her body shaking. The idea of standing up to Doreen seemed to scare her. I decided not to offer Kwanele any of my items.

"I'll get it back from her myself."

As I watched Kwanele walk away, my chest rose and fell over and over, as if I'd been doing tiring exercises. I clenched my hands and took a deep breath.

"It'll be okay," Thabisa said when I told her what happened.

I sniffled. "Doreen is so mean and Kwanele is fake."

"Don't worry about it now. Let's hurry to class or else we'll be late."

Mrs. Moya had already arrived so I didn't have a chance to talk to Doreen until lunch break. I went to Doreen's desk before Doreen left the classroom.

"Can I have my book back? I know what happened," I said to her. My chest was heaving even though I was trying hard not to show her how upset I was.

Doreen smirked. "I don't know what you're talking about."

"Kwanele told me what happened. I confronted her."

"Listen." She laid her hands on my shoulders and squeezed them hard. "You don't own the book and have no right to keep it forever."

"Never lay a hand on me again or else I'll tell the

headmistress and you'll be expelled from school." I pushed away her hands.

"Is that a threat?"

I dropped my backpack, but I didn't bend to pick it up right away. "I'm the one who checked the book out of the library. You used Kwanele to get the book. You shouldn't have done that." I clamped my mouth shut and stood tall.

Doreen narrowed her eyes. "You're really trying to be tough, aren't you? I can't believe you're telling me what I can or can't do. If you want the book so bad, I'll return it to you."

"When?"

"I'll bring it tomorrow, okay? You better not tell Mrs. Moya about this. Otherwise, I'll tell her you're lying and no one will believe you." Doreen stood from her chair and hurried out of the classroom. She seemed unwilling to change.

As I walked toward Thabisa, I thought about my conversation with Doreen. Would Doreen return the library book? I'd expected her to refuse to give the book back. But if I didn't get a copy of Cinderella and lost my role in the play, I might ruin my chance to be known as the girl who made the trip a success.

Chapter 9

On the way home, I saw pieces of paper strewn under a Jacaranda tree. Someone had torn down a poster. I cried out and covered my mouth with my hand. More ripped posters lay scattered on the streets Thabisa and I passed.

"I can't believe this has happened." I breathed heavily. "Do you think Doreen has something to do with this? What if she and Ntando tear up every single poster? We've worked so hard." I bent down to pick up a piece of paper.

Thabisa patted my back. "I'm sorry. Whoever did it is very wrong."

I said, "I wouldn't be surprised if Kwanele is involved. We'll have to think of another plan."

The next day I didn't get a chance to confront Doreen about my library book until the bell rang for lunch break. I waited for her at our classroom door. When she walked right past me, I tugged at her shoulder. She turned around and glared at me.

"What?" she spat the words out.

"Do you have the library book? I need to practice."

Doreen folded her arms and creased her forehead. "I'll give it to you tomorrow, okay."

"Make sure you do so. I haven't practiced at all."

"That's not my fault."

"You should keep your promises."

"I said tomorrow. Now I need to eat my lunch." Doreen spun around and walked toward Ntando.

Thabisa stood under the Jacaranda tree waiting for me. The sunlight filtered through the branches, warming my face. The breeze fluttered leaves gently, but they were starting to turn from green to brown since it hadn't rained for several days.

"I saw you talking to Doreen. Is everything all right?" Thabisa asked, sitting on the bench.

I nodded and told Thabisa about my conversation with Doreen.

Thabisa crossed her arms over her lap. "I'll help you once you get the book. We'll read together."

"Thank you. But you can't memorize my lines for me," I said. "I just thought of a plan. Why don't we make flyers announcing the play and stick them in people's mailboxes."

Thabisa grinned. "Good idea. You're the best!"

We talked more about the play. Thabisa smiled when she talked about appearing at Cinderella's wedding. Her eyes remained bright as I mentioned that I was excited to be Cinderella. After eating, we went to the library hoping a copy of the play had been returned, but the other two books were still checked out.

I confronted Doreen about my library book before classes started the next day.

"I forgot it at home. I'll bring it tomorrow," Doreen said, smirking.

"Why don't you write a note so you remember?" I said. If I didn't get the book soon, I'd be in trouble with Mrs. Moya. I'd be forced to tell her the truth even though she didn't like excuses.

"Why don't you let me walk home with you, then I'll get the book?" I said.

Doreen glanced at me sideways. "You're not welcome to my house. Wait till tomorrow, okay."

"Make sure you bring it then."

Doreen didn't bring the book the next day or the day after. I was more worried about not knowing my lines than about having to pay for the book. When I was about to tell the teacher I didn't have a book, I noticed Vumani, the boy playing the prince, reading the *Cinderella* play. I thought of an idea.

"Hi, can I borrow your book for a few days?" I said. Maybe it was better not to involve Mrs. Moya if possible.

"Where's your copy?" He flipped to another page.

I cleared my throat. "I don't have it. I'll return your book as soon as I finish."

Vumani handed me the book. "You can keep it for now, but give it back to me after the rehearsal."

I wanted to hug him. "Thank you so much!" I smiled. Doreen and her friends groaned, but I pretended I couldn't hear them. How could they try to spoil my day and what could be a good year?

During lunch break, I practiced my lines. " 'Um, I'll mak-k-ke your break breakfast...' " I stopped. "Why am I so nervous and why don't the words come out easily?"

Thabisa patted my arm. "Keep reading. You'll be fine. I know you can do it."

"If I could block our classmates from my head I'd learn better." I felt that if I didn't learn my lines I'd fail and my enemies would win. "When I'm nervous, I have trouble memorizing anything. If I could memorize I'd be a better student. I wish I didn't get nervous easily. Sometimes I think I'm not normal because I have so much trouble memorizing."

"Of course, you're normal. Don't think like that."

At home, I rushed to my bedroom without eating and started practicing.

" 'I didn't want to disturb you while you were sleeping,' " I read a line I'd address to Doreen, the stepmother. I shivered at the thought of giving in to the stepmother's wishes. Doreen must love her role.

"Try to repeat your lines without looking," Thabisa said. "I'll help you."

I nodded, but when I tried to recite the lines, my mind went blank. " 'I didn't want to disturb, to disturb...' " I shook my head. "I can't."

"Try again."

" 'I didn't want to disturb you because you were sleeping.' "

68

"Good job. Close enough," Thabisa said. "Keep going."

But I couldn't remember the next few Cinderella lines. I bit my lip, my eyes watering at the thought of not being part of the play. My ability to change my voice wasn't going to work in my favor if I couldn't even memorize my lines.

Chapter 10

On the day I expected Grandma to come home, Thabisa and I baked a cake for her and made a poster that read, "Get Well Soon." MaSibanda helped us clean Grandma's room and change the sheets.

Mama arrived with Grandma by taxi. I ran outside and hugged Grandma, then I gripped Mama's waist and cried out. Tears streamed down my face as Mama and I hugged. When she let me loose, I gazed at her. Her curly hair reached her shoulders, her face had no makeup, and her lips shone as if she'd smeared lip balm on them. She wore pants which were flared at the bottom. In two years, she hadn't changed much.

"Oh, Busisiwe. I missed you so. I love you very much." Mama patted my head with her palm.

"I missed you and I love you too, Mama," I said, clinging to her.

"I just told your mother that you look very much like her," Grandma said, leaning on her cane, her back more hunched than before. Her voice was back to normal, but her face seemed more wrinkled than when she was admitted to the hospital.

"I'm glad you're feeling better, Grandma," I said.

"I am fine." Grandma turned to Mama. "There

was no reason for you to miss work, my daughter. But I am also very happy to see you," she said. "And you too, my grandchild."

Mama and I held on to Grandma as we shuffled into the house, where Thabisa and her mother waited. After they greeted Mama and wished Grandma well, Thabisa and her mother got ready to leave, but Mama asked them to stay for dinner.

While eating, Mama talked about her flight from the U.S.A.

"I was lucky I got a cheap ticket to come here. My employer is so understanding." Mama poured water into a glass. "The food tastes great. I'm used to eating in a hurry. I hardly ever sit down for a proper meal."

"My granddaughter will be in a school play," Grandma said. "I am proud."

"Wonderful," Mama said. "What's the name of the play?"

I wiped my mouth with my hands. "*Cinderella.* Guess what? I'm playing Cinderella."

"How nice that you'll have the lead role! I wish I could see the play." Mama swirled the water in her glass.

"We'll take pictures and send them to you," I said.

"How are your classes going?" Mama asked. I had expected that question.

"Okay. We've only just started. I think I'll do better this year," I said. I decided to drop the topic, not wanting to discuss my school performance.

"Grandma is related to Thabisa's mother."

"That is so true," Grandma said. "She is a Sibanda and from Khezi."

"I'm happy we met, my sister," Mama said to MaSibanda. I smiled because Mama and Grandma treated MaSibanda and Thabisa like close family.

"Busi has been very good to Thabisa. I'm glad our daughters became friends fast," MaSibanda said.

Mama nodded. "I am too."

She talked about her job and undergraduate school. Life seemed very different in Texas. Did Mama ever have time for fun since she went to college during the day and worked too? On weekends, she worked twelve hours or more a day, but that didn't make me change my mind about living in the U.S.A. some day.

"We better go back to the Nalas," MaSibanda said after she finished eating and helping clean up. "I know you want to rest after your long trip."

"You're welcome to stay longer. Thank you for staying with my daughter," Mama said.

"We'll visit sometime," MaSibanda said.

"Thanks for everything," I said. "I'm glad you stayed with me. I wouldn't have been comfortable staying in the house alone."

"You're good people. You and the Nalas are very kind," Grandma said.

"I owe you a lot for being so good to my family." Mama shook MaSibanda's hand.

"See you at school, Busi," Thabisa said.

After Thabisa and her mother left, Mama and I sat next to Grandma. Grandma's eyes seemed brighter than they were the day before and she kept her gaze on Mama. My heart warmed because Grandma was in such good spirits and her health had improved. I updated Mama on what had been happening since she last called. Mama told me that my CDs were still on the way and that I'd get them soon. Afterwards, I retrieved my music box from my room and showed it to Mama.

"It's as lovely as you described it," Mama said.

I nodded. "Every time I listen to it, I'm reminded of Florence. I play it every day before bedtime. It's really comforting. I just believe I sleep better when I know that the next day I'll see it when I wake up. I play it while getting ready for school too."

"You are a lucky girl to get something of great sentimental value from a friend. Just remember you have friends who are real."

"I hope I see Florence again. She, Thabisa, and I could have so much fun together," I said.

The music trilling reminded me how lucky I was Grandma had survived the stroke and that Mama was home for a visit.

"I wish you could both come with me to the U.S.," Mama said. "But I'm not a citizen and don't even have a green card. How can I leave you two alone?"

"I wish I could come with you, too, Mama. And

with Grandma, too, of course."

I frowned at the thought of not going to the U.S.A. with Mama. I'd miss her so much. But deep down I knew I could never leave Grandma behind.

"When I'm gone, you'll need someone else to stay with you. You need help around the house."

"Why don't we ask Thabisa and her mother to stay with us? They have really been good to me," I said.

Mama sighed. "They have their own lives though, you know."

"Please talk to them. You don't mind them staying here. Do you, Grandma?"

Grandma shook her head. "If that is what you wish. Maybe your mama is right. If something happened to me, what would you do? Maybe MaSibanda will like to stay here. I know you would love to be with Thabisa."

"I'll have to decide whether to call them," Mama said. "I'll start calling relatives to find out if there's anyone who can stay with you after I'm gone."

I rose and held Grandma's hand, then I washed the dishes while listening to my music box and humming the song "Forever Your Friend."

Chapter 11

Two days before the rehearsal, Doreen plopped my book on top of my desk soon after she arrived at school. I gasped when I noticed that my book now had bent edges and looked faded as if it had been dumped in water, then dried in the sun. How could Doreen have been so careless with a library book? Did she damage it on purpose?

"Say something. I brought your book back." Doreen smirked. "Don't I deserve a 'thank you'?"

"You shouldn't have done that to my book. It's wrong." Without waiting for a response, I headed to the classroom to tell Mrs. Moya what Doreen had done.

I wished Doreen would take responsibility for her actions. She had gone too far and Mrs. Moya needed to know about the incident. But when the teacher arrived that day, she started teaching without even calling the roll. I approached Mrs. Moya during lunch break.

"I'm busy grading and I can only talk if this is an emergency," she said without looking up.

What Doreen did was wrong and could get her in trouble. But was it urgent news? Anyway, this time Doreen hadn't laid a finger on me.

"I'll come back later," I said. The teacher didn't seem to notice that I was upset. Maybe I'd give up talking to her that day.

I flipped through the pages of my book and was relieved that they were easy to read. Now that I had my book back, I returned Vumani's and thanked him.

When I reached home, I explained to Mama what happened to my library book.

"That's awful. Why didn't you tell me that this girl took your book sooner?" Mama's forehead furrowed.

I shrugged. "Another classmate lent me a book. Anyway, you've got enough worries for now." Tears welled up in my eyes. I was with Mama after all, so I didn't have to hide my feelings.

Mama squeezed my shoulder. "Oh, Busisiwe. You know you can always open up to me. I'll go and talk to your teacher about this. You shouldn't have to pay for the damage done to the book."

"Please don't, Mama. My classmates will hate me for it."

"No one in her right mind would hate you for doing what's right."

I shook my head. "You don't understand, Mama. The girls can be really mean."

"Let me handle this, okay," Mama said, and I decided that arguing with her would be a waste of time.

I went to my room and practiced the lines I had

the most trouble with even before working on my homework. I silently read the stepsisters' lines.

Cinderella, you didn't iron any clothes for me to wear. I have to wear these wrinkled ones!

I want you to go and make my bed right away!

I let out a deep breath, then I recited Cinderella's lines. " 'What about breakfast?' "

My fingers shook as I read my lines. It normally took me weeks to memorize several lines, so I was nervous. Mama tried to help, but she had to stop reading several times to help Grandma with her daily activities.

The next afternoon, Mama arrived in my classroom as soon as the bell rang to announce the end of the school day. All of my classmates were still there, but they were getting ready to leave for their homes. I tapped on my desk with my fingers and tried not to look up at Mama. The last thing I wanted was for Mama to confront Doreen or talk to Mrs. Moya about the library book in front of the whole class.

"This is Busi's mother, everyone. Say hello." Mrs. Moya smiled as if she'd been offered a precious gift.

A few of my classmates muttered, "Hello," but most of them kept quiet. When my eyes met Doreen's, I cringed. How was I going to win my classmates' favor now? Doreen would definitely try to get back at me for having Mama come all the way to school to complain about the library book. Mrs. Moya dismissed the class and only Doreen and I remained. I hoped to hear exactly what Mama had to say.

"I said you're all dismissed," Mrs. Moya said through clenched teeth so I had to guess what she was saying. I hesitated, but when Mrs. Moya shooed me away, I picked up my backpack and left the class-room, keeping my distance from Doreen.

The next day Mrs. Moya called Doreen and Ntando to the front of the class before teaching. I sucked in my breath. I knew why she was calling the girls. The idea of Doreen and Ntando getting in trouble made me sigh with relief, but my heart couldn't help pounding. Whose side would my classmates take?

"Do you know why I called you?" Mrs. Moya asked.

"No, ma'am," Doreen said, looking the teacher in the eye.

"Tell me why you stole Busi's library book and ruined it."

"But, we didn't steal it," Ntando said.

"Do you know that you could be suspended for stealing something that belongs to the school? Tell me everything. I want the complete truth." Mrs. Moya's brow furrowed.

Doreen turned around and pointed toward Kwanele. "Kwanele gave me the book."

"Kwanele come to the front and explain how you're involved."

Kwanele shuffled to the front of the classroom. Her eyes brimmed with tears and she kept her head bent.

Kwanele looked at Doreen, her head cocked. "I'm sorry."

"Talk to me, not Doreen," Mrs. Moya said.

"I asked Busi for the book because..."

"Continue."

"Doreen made me." Kwanele burst into tears and her nose started running. I couldn't help feeling sorry for her.

"I'm going to postpone the rehearsal until next week," Mrs. Moya said. "The three of you are getting detention for the next four Fridays. If you break the school rules again, you won't take part in the school play. I'll cancel the trip if I have to."

My classmates remained quiet, so I didn't know if they were angry with Doreen for trying to ruin the trip or with me for telling my mother what Doreen and Ntando had done. I couldn't help sympathizing with Kwanele who was still sobbing. But I tried to cheer up when I realized I had more time to learn my lines.

Chapter 12

I dreaded entering the classroom the next day because I'd gotten Doreen and Ntando in trouble. I avoided eye contact with Doreen and slumped in my chair. While I was chatting with Thabisa, something struck the back of my head. When I turned around, I noticed that Doreen and Ntando were laughing. They'd thrown a plastic ball the size of a fist at me and it had rolled to the front of the classroom. None of the other students said anything and Thabisa gasped.

Doreen picked up the ball and shook it at me. "How would you like to spend your Friday afternoon picking up thrash? Do you really think you can get away with what you did? You don't know how to stand up for yourself. You just run to your mother."

I squared my shoulders. "It's your fault—not my fault—that you have detention."

"You think you can get away with anything. You think you're all that."

"You're wrong about me, Doreen. I'm not different from anyone else. I just want you to treat me fairly."

"I won't let you get away with this. You better stay behind every Friday too or else you'll be sorry,"

Doreen said and quickly walked to her desk when Mrs. Moya entered the classroom.

After school, Mama and I walked in the neighborhood while Grandma napped. Our arms were linked. That day, more people than usual sat on mats in the shade selling bags of sweets, tomatoes, and fruits. Minty aromas filled the air. Children stopped to buy sweets, then they chased one another, laughing and hollering. The sun blazed and I constantly shielded my face.

"I'm glad you made friends fast. I know you miss Florence," Mama said.

"I do wish she were still here. Then I'd have two good friends." I wanted to tell Mama what happened in class today, but I changed my mind. What if Mama went back to talk to Mrs. Moya about Doreen's behavior?

"I was lucky to have even one friend in primary and secondary school. I wasn't outgoing and neither was your grandma as a child."

"Why does the same thing happen to us?" I asked.

"All I can say is that we're a shy family and have to work harder to be recognized."

"How did you deal with bullies?"

"I didn't. In fact, the girls in my school took advantage of me because I was shy. I never stood up for myself and I should have." Mama paused. "Are the others really being mean to you, Busisiwe? I imagine you're not telling me everything."

"I'm okay. At least I have Thabisa."

"I know things will be different for you. You're strong and can stand up for yourself. You won't make the same mistakes I did." Mama put an arm around me.

I wanted to ask her how I should handle Doreen, but I decided not to worry her. I would figure out the best way to stop the bullying on my own.

Mama stopped to admire a knitted rug a woman was selling. I picked up the rug and unfolded it. "Grandma liked to travel a lot. She took me everywhere," I said. I laid the rug back down.

"She became more outgoing as she grew older. I did, so you should, too."

"I think if I didn't have friends I'd listen to music all day long," I said. "Sometimes I do wish everyone liked me, but maybe I'm asking too much."

"You *are* very likable. Florence and Thabisa are lucky to have a friend like you."

"I wonder if I'll hear from Florence again."

We spent the next hour looking at the goods the vendors were selling and Mama bought the knitted rug. Afterwards, we explored the neighborhood. Most of the yards we passed had identical flat-roofed houses and mulberry, guava, and peach trees. We reached the park where clumps of grass had turned yellow. A few children were playing dodgeball in the park. A swing and a seesaw stood in the middle of the park reminding me of the days I used to play there.

"Mama, would you consider moving back here?" I asked as she perched on a bench in the shade.

Mama sat next to me and nodded. "I think about it all the time, but I need to get a good education so I can get a job to support you."

"What about Dad?" I asked. "He sometimes sends me presents for my birthday, but I wonder if he does that because he feels he has to."

"Your father works hard. Give him time."

I picked up a twig, snapped it in half, flung it on the ground, and stamped my feet. "Mama, how long should I wait? Does he only care about his work and his other family?"

"Calm down now." Mama put her arm around me. "He *does* care. You're his daughter."

"What will happen when he has other children? Will he forget about me completely?" I asked. "I do love him, and wish he could visit."

"Call him. Let him know how you feel."

"I called him recently."

"Give him time, he'll call back."

"I was just thinking how other kids at school live with their parents. Maybe that's one of the reasons I feel out of place," I said. I sighed, feeling like I'd unloaded a burden.

"You could visit me sometime. Your grandmother might refuse to visit me though."

I sniffed. "I do want to. Grandma would have to come too."

Mama took my hand in hers. "I think about you all the time, my daughter. I work hard for you."

"I know."

We sat in the park longer, then we left in silence. For the first time since Mama visited, I had asked her about Dad. Why did she come up with excuses each time I asked her about him and why didn't she criticize him for neglecting me? Even before she and Dad separated, Mama didn't complain and always told me to be patient and that things would work out. Eventually, Dad moved out of our house in Bulawayo and didn't visit until I begged him to.

"Mama, are you going to talk to Thabisa and her mom about moving in with Grandma and me?" I asked as we headed home.

"Are you sure that's what you want?"

I nodded. "I'd love to spend time with Thabisa every day. Grandma could also use extra help."

"Okay. I'll talk to them. I called your uncles in Bulawayo to ask them if they knew anyone looking for work. So far, I haven't heard anything and I'll be leaving soon. But remember Thabisa and her mother might already have other plans."

"Oh, thanks, Mama. I'm so excited!" I hoped MaSibanda would agree to be a housekeeper.

Chapter 13

Two days before Mama returned to the U.S.A., she and I went to the Nalas and invited Thabisa and her mother to dinner. During dinner, Mama explained that she wished MaSibanda and Thabisa could live with me and Grandma.

"Sweets haven't been selling well lately," MaSibanda said. "So we'd be happy to stay with Grandma and Busi again. I was worried about how we'd pay rent and school fees."

I looked up from my plate and grinned.

"I'm so glad you're willing to stay with my mother and daughter." Mama unfurled a napkin. "Thank you. You're family after all. I know my mother will be in good hands."

She offered to give MaSibanda a monthly salary. Grandma and I would share food with Thabisa and her mother. The news made me smile.

"I'm excited you'll be living here, Thabisa. We'll have so much fun," I said, my eyes bright.

"Me too. I can't wait to move in again," Thabisa said. Food spilled from her mouth as she giggled.

"My granddaughter will have someone to spend time with." Grandma patted my shoulder. "She needs a friend."

I wanted to give all the clothes that were too tight for me to Thabisa. Now that we'd be living together, I'd treat her like a sister. Maybe if I treated her like family, she would be less likely to think I gave her clothes because she was poor.

The next morning Thabisa and her mother moved their stuff to Grandma's house. Clothes packed in boxes were soon stacked in the spare bedroom. I helped Thabisa pack dishes, pots, and pans in the kitchen cupboard, then Mama and I helped Grandma get out of bed and get dressed. After being confined to the hospital, Grandma needed personal assistance and she struggled to walk around the house.

"You should try to walk every day, Mother. Exercise will help you get strong again," Mama said, holding Grandma's right arm. I grasped Grandma's left arm.

"I am trying. I'll be running very soon, even before you go back to America." Grandma smiled. I realized that she laughed more and her eyes were livelier now that she was home and Mama was back. Seeing Grandma happy made my heart flutter with joy. Mama and I walked with Grandma in the front yard, stopping often to take breaks.

While Grandma hobbled about the house, clutching her cane, I walked beside her. When Grandma tried to help with cooking and cleaning, MaSibanda begged her to sit down and rest.

That night, Grandma went to bed earlier than usual, saying that the walk had worn her out. Mama slept in my bedroom and we checked on Grandma a few times at night.

"Mother is doing so much better. You're taking good care of her," Mama said after she and I returned from Grandma's room. Mama sat on her bed, stretched her arms, and yawned.

I sat next to Mama and leaned my head against her. "I'm not doing much really. I worry about Grandma sometimes and can't fall asleep easily."

Mama stroked my hair. "I know it's hard to sleep when you've a lot on your mind, but try to rest. I have a hard time sleeping when I have classes or work the next day."

"Do you mind if I play my music box? I'm not sleepy."

"Not at all, but don't stay up too late," Mama said. "I'm going to try to sleep now. You don't have to turn off the lights right away."

I played my music box quietly looking back at the days I'd spent with Mama, and wanting time to slow down. In a few days, Mama would be leaving, but life would continue.

On the day Mama was leaving, I rode a taxi with her and Grandma, and we headed to the airport. I kissed Mama on both cheeks and hugged her tight, my eyes glistening with tears.

"Bye, Mama. I'll miss you," I said when it was

time for Mama to board the plane. "I wish you didn't have to leave so soon."

"Bye, I'll miss you too, Busisiwe." Mama turned to Grandma. "Stay in good health, Mother. I'll miss both of you."

"I will think of you, my daughter," Grandma said.

"Please call often and give my love to Dad," I said. A tear trickled down my face.

"I will, goodbye."

As Grandma and I waved to Mama, I wondered if I'd see Mama again anytime soon. Although part of me wished I could join Mama, deep down I had few other regrets. I couldn't leave Grandma, even to be with Mama. Besides, I'd made friends with Thabisa.

When we returned home, I went to my room and lay on my bed, wanting to be alone. I held my music box against my chest and felt less lonely. Thabisa shared a room with her mother as she did when Grandma was in the hospital. Grandma and I each had our own room. I had suggested Thabisa share a room with me, but she'd refused saying she wanted me to have some privacy. Ever since Mama had moved to the U.S.A., no relatives had visited for more than a few days. Most of them were in Bulawayo and owned homes. Life would be different now that I had more company.

I already missed Mama. When she first went to the U.S.A., I had cried at the airport too. Seeing her depart two years later reminded me I couldn't always be with everyone I cared about at the same time. I was grateful Grandma was with me and as I recalled the day I'd found her on the kitchen floor, my heart thumped. When I listened to the CDs my parents bought me, I'd think of them, as I sometimes thought of Florence when I listened to the music box. More than any of my items, my family and friends made me happy. But the gifts they showered me with were sometimes the only things that stayed with me permanently.

The last time I saw my father was when he came to Zimbabwe two years ago. Thabisa and I hadn't spoken about our fathers. Where was Thabisa's?

Thabisa was in the sitting room watching TV.

"I haven't heard from my father for weeks now," I said as I sat on the sofa next to Thabisa. "I'm beginning to wonder if he cares about me."

"I haven't seen mine for years," Thabisa said without looking at me. "I don't think he cares about me. I don't like to talk about him."

"I'm sorry. That must be hard."

"It's okay. If I get married it will be forever. It's been very difficult without my father around."

"Same here," I said. "My parents didn't get along most of the time. I miss Dad though and Mama too, of course."

"I miss my brothers. Sometimes I wish I lived with them and my grandparents in the country." Thabisa rested her leg on the table.

"Do you visit them every holiday?"

Thabisa nodded. "I spend all my vacations in the country with my relatives. We have so much fun together."

"I wish I had brothers and sisters. It's not easy being an only child sometimes," I said.

We stared at the TV screen, but I guessed neither of us was watching the show. I realized Thabisa and I had something else in common besides the way our classmates treated us. Hopefully, their attitude would change.

Chapter 14

An hour before the end of the school day, Mrs. Moya told me and my classmates to rehearse. I shuffled to the front of the classroom, reluctant to recite my lines in front of my classmates. I wished I'd already memorized my lines.

"Act lively," Mrs. Moya said. "This is not the time to be shy. If you can't perform in front of your classmates, how are you going to perform in front of strangers? Show me what you can do."

" 'Wake up, Cinderella...!' " Doreen yelled her lines.

"Stop," Mrs. Moya said. "Be firm, but don't yell. There will be a big audience, but everyone will hear you as long as you speak clearly."

When Doreen narrowed her eyes at me, I remained silent. I resolved not to let her or any of my classmates get on my nerves.

"Busi, say your line," Mrs. Moya said.

"I'll make your break-k-k..."

Doreen covered her mouth with her hand to stifle laughter. Soon the majority of my classmates joined in laughing. I kept my head high and tried to stay calm.

"Silence." Mrs. Moya rapped on the table with her

ruler. "This is not a game. Don't you want to go on the school trip?" When no one answered, Mrs. Moya continued. "Say your lines again, Busi."

I tried to recite my lines, but I started sweating even though the room wasn't that hot. Why did I forget my lines so easily?

When I tried to recite my lines again, I stuttered.

"I'll allow you to look at the script today, but next time you must know your lines," Mrs. Moya said and I sighed with relief.

"I already know my lines, ma'am," Doreen said.

"Good. Just have the script in front of you in case you forget any lines."

The rehearsal continued and I was more confident now that I had the script. Doreen continued to yell, not hiding her dislike for me, and Mrs. Moya interrupted the rehearsal a few times. I thought my voice was sweet compared to Doreen's. When Mrs. Moya finally dismissed the class, I thought I had performed well.

When I arrived home, I headed to Grandma's room, only to find her sleeping. Afterwards, I went straight to my bedroom and changed. Thabisa entered the room half an hour later.

"You performed well today," she said.

"Thanks," I said. "I'm lucky Mrs. Moya let me look at the book. What would I have done if she'd given the role to someone else right away?"

"You'll be all right," Thabisa said. "You've time to

memorize your lines."

"I don't know. I'm really slow at memorizing. I'm trying not to let Doreen upset me, but it's hard."

"Just think of the positive things, like the good time we'll have together at Vic Falls."

"I'll try." I smiled.

After Thabisa left, I flipped the music box open. As the music rang in my ears, I closed my eyes and swayed to the music, lost in another world where I imagined myself as Cinderella. Then I walked to the kitchen, where MaSibanda and Thabisa were putting away groceries. When I greeted her, MaSibanda smiled. I helped with the groceries and afterwards, we pulled out chairs and sat down.

"How was school, Busi?" MaSibanda said.

"It was okay," I said.

I sighed with relief when she didn't push me to talk more about my day. I didn't want to think about Doreen or my classmates now.

When Grandma entered the room, I pulled out a chair for her, smiling. I decided she wasn't going anywhere that afternoon because her head was uncovered and she wore her sleeveless nightgown. But her legs were steadier and her smile was back to normal. After she sat down, I hugged her and squeezed her wrinkled hands, which felt warm.

"I have been sleeping for a long time. I can't stay awake these days," Grandma said.

"Would you like something to drink, Grandma?"

I asked. I put my arm over Grandma's chair.

"You can make tea."

I poured water in a kettle while Thabisa set the table before serving meat pies.

"The term will be over before you girls know it," MaSibanda said. "Are you ready for your play?"

I shook my head. "I don't even know my lines well yet, but I've been practicing."

"Do you have enough time?" Grandma asked.

"I think so," I said even though I was concerned that time was moving too fast.

"Just make sure you do your school work first," Grandma said.

After we finished eating, Thabisa and I went to the living room and did homework. Then I lay down on the carpet and read the *Cinderella* play. Thabisa sat on a chair reading a novel. Although I had read *Cinderella* before, I still struggled to memorize the play word for word. If I was playing the fairy godmother I'd have fewer lines to practice. After reading for about half an hour without making progress, I decided to take a break. Thabisa seemed absorbed in her novel.

When I tried reading the play in my room that night, I yawned. I put it aside so I could try again tomorrow on Thursday. How was I going to pass grade six if I had trouble memorizing anything?

The following day, when I approached the classroom with Thabisa, some of my classmates were standing outside in groups. They giggled as Thabisa and I walked into the classroom. I wished Mrs. Moya would show up and give them detention. I squared my shoulders as I settled next to Thabisa.

After the bell rang, my classmates returned to the classroom.

"Cinderella should be played by someone else," Doreen said as soon as she settled in her seat. "Mrs. Moya isn't fair sometimes. Busi doesn't know how to act. She can never remember her lines, but she's been given enough chances to practice."

"She and Thabisa still don't get why no one likes them. They get on my nerves," Ntando said.

I pretended I wasn't listening to the conversation. There was nothing new in what Doreen and Ntando were saying about me. Since they hadn't physically tried to hurt me, I didn't care what they said about me. Thabisa continued reading as if she hadn't even heard their conversation.

I was grateful when Mrs. Moya arrived and silenced the class. At lunchtime, I sat with Thabisa in the shade. Today the schoolyard smelled of freshly cut grass. The air was dry, and the sunlight filtering through the branches didn't bother me.

"We really deserve more credit," I said, trying not to sound irritable. "We came up with the idea of playing Cinderella and I'll lend our classmates clothes for the play, but they don't seem to care. Maybe if I start talking to the others more, they'll come around. I'll also try to be more cheerful in school."

"They will change," Thabisa said. "It hurts the way they treat us sometimes, but if we allow them to get on our nerves, we'll be miserable."

"I know. I'll stop worrying about what they think."

"I've been through a lot in my life, so I try to ignore mean people," Thabisa said. "I've been mistreated a lot in schools before. One day I got into a fight with a boy and I got in trouble with the teacher. My mother gave me a lecture and I had to change."

"I can't imagine you fighting. You're so gentle."

"I've changed really."

"I know we'll always be friends," I said. "As long as we have each other, it doesn't matter what others think."

After school, Thabisa and I went straight home. I found a package from Mama in my room and ripped it open to reveal the CDs she had promised me. I cried out, then Thabisa and I sang "Forever Your Friend." Now I could expand my CD collection! The CDs made up for my lousy day and all the awful things my classmates had said.

In the sitting room, Grandma leaned back in her chair, clutching her cane. I plopped on the sofa next to her and crossed my legs.

"You look great, Grandma," I said.

"I feel very good because you're here." Grandma's eyes shone and she seemed to have fewer wrinkles on her face.

I grinned. "I'm thrilled to be with you too."

"Seeing you happy makes me happy. You have changed since Thabisa came. I knew you were lonely."

"I don't know what I'd do without Thabisa," I said. "I always enjoy your company, of course."

What mattered to me the most was being around those I loved. Popularity wasn't important after all. Tomorrow I'd be more positive in school and hopefully be happier there even if I only had a few friends.

Chapter 15

That Friday, Mrs. Moya told our class we'd be re-hearsing *Cinderella* again the following Monday. February had arrived and the play was a month away.

My heart thumped. "Ma'am, please postpone the rehearsal. I need more time," I said.

"But you've had weeks to practice." Mrs. Moya struck her table with her ruler. "Do you want to be Cinderella or not?"

"I do, ma'am," I said.

"Then go practice your lines and be ready for the rehearsal."

When I stepped outside, Doreen stood at the door holding the *Cinderella* play. Kwanele and her friends were nearby.

"Let me hear you say your lines, Cinderella," Doreen said.

"I can't talk now, Doreen."

Kwanele and other classmates stared at me as if waiting to see how I reacted.

"Why not?" Doreen asked.

"Have fun learning your lines, Doreen." I looked Doreen in the eyes and smiled, not caring what any-one thought of me. When I glanced at Kwanele and her friends, I noticed they were smiling too.

I turned toward Thabisa who stood under a Jacaranda tree waiting for me.

"I saw you talking to Doreen. Is everything all right?" Thabisa asked.

I sat on the grass, and she joined me. "Yes, everything is fine. I just wish I knew my lines."

Thabisa crossed an arm over her lap. "I'll help you this weekend. We'll read together."

"I wish you could memorize my lines for me. You're really good at it," I said.

We pulled out chicken sandwiches from our bags. While we were eating, I spotted Vumani sitting with his friends on a bench and he waved at me, grinning. Was he really trying to be friendly? I waved back and smiled. He whispered something to his friends, then he stood up and walked toward me and Thabisa.

"How are you, Busi?" His voice was gentle and I could tell he wasn't making fun of me like Doreen.

"Good. You?"

"I couldn't be better," Vumani said. "Are you girls ready for the play?"

"Not yet. I still have to practice my lines."

"You'll do fine," he said. "Don't let anyone tell you that you can't do it."

I grinned as he turned and walked away. He'd approached me for the first time. Maybe everyone noticed I was making an effort to stay in a good mood. I pulled out the *Cinderella* play from my bag so I could practice my lines before I returned to the classroom. Could I really memorize them in a few days and still do my homework? Homework usually took me hours to complete. I'd better learn my lines otherwise Doreen would continue to make fun of me.

"Can you play the fairy godmother to help me practice?" I flipped the book open.

"Sure," Thabisa said. She ran a finger along the page and read a line. " 'I can make your wishes come true, Cinderella.' "

" 'I wish I could go to the ball, but I don't have any nice clothes. Why would the prince choose to dance with me?' " I said. "How do I sound?"

"I think you sound good, but a little nervous," Thabisa said. "Maybe you could slow down a little. Keep reading. You can do it."

The bell rang before I could read more pages. In class, I thought about my lines, but I remembered only the first few. Mrs. Moya gave us more homework than usual and ignored those who groaned.

At home, I rushed to my room without eating and started practicing. Each time I tried to recite my lines without looking at my book, my mind went blank.

Someone knocked on the door. I opened it. Thabisa entered the bedroom holding a glass of water.

"This is for you." She handed me the cup. "You should drink something."

"Thanks. I still don't know my lines. Will I be able to be part of the play?"

"You have the weekend. You can do it."

On Saturday, I spent hours doing my homework and I didn't have time to read the play. The next day I struggled to memorize my lines.

That night I couldn't fall asleep so I went to the sitting room where I had left the copy of the play and found Thabisa there reading it. I peered over her shoulder and she shuddered as if she was startled. I knelt on the floor beside her.

"I didn't see you come in." Thabisa scratched her head.

"Sorry, I didn't want to disturb you."

"I've been reading Cinderella lines for fun. But I'm coming to bed now." Thabisa handed the book to me and I took it and opened the first page with text. "Aren't you tired?" she asked.

"I am, but I really want to be Cinderella. She's such a great character to play and I really want Grandma to see me acting throughout the play," I said.

"I'll stay up with you. I'm not tired yet."

We read *Cinderella* together and went to bed after midnight. I dreamed I had stage fright and fainted in the middle of the play.

On Monday morning, I awoke drenched in sweat.

While bathing, I tried to recite my lines, but I stumbled over and over. After I finished bathing, I read my book and flipped to the page with the lines I found hard to remember.

After breakfast, I hurried out the door. "Today's rehearsal day and I don't even know my lines!"

Chapter 16

When Thabisa and I arrived at school, the morning bell had rung. As soon as we walked into the classroom, everyone else was there and Mrs. Moya was already teaching. Why did we have to be so late on rehearsal day? I hoped Mrs. Moya would forgive us.

"Sorry, I'm late, ma'am," I said after Mrs. Moya stopped talking.

"Sorry, I'm late," Thabisa said.

Mrs. Moya continued teaching without replying. I sat down in my chair and yanked my notebook from my backpack.

While Mrs. Moya taught Math problems, I thought about Cinderella lines, but I only remembered my dialogue with the fairy godmother.

"Turn to page forty-seven and work on the first exercise," Mrs. Moya said. "After lunch, we'll rehearse." She sat down and opened the *Cinderella* play.

Since Mrs. Moya wasn't watching me, I decided to read *Cinderella* too. I pulled the play from my backpack, laid it on top of my mathematics book, and pretended to write in my notebook.

"Busi," Mrs. Moya called out minutes later. I almost jumped in my seat. "Can you come to the board and answer the first problem?"

I shut the *Cinderella* play. Mrs. Moya came over to my desk.

"You aren't working on the exercises?" Mrs. Moya wagged a finger at me. "Why didn't you do what I asked you to?"

"Sorry, ma'am," I said, my hands shaking.

"Do you ever listen?" Mrs. Moya creased her forehead. "Next time you'll answer to the headmistress."

I kept quiet and tried not to look her in the eyes.

"Give me that book," Mrs. Moya said.

I handed *Cinderella* to Mrs. Moya. None of my classmates said anything.

"Go to the board and solve the problem now," Mrs. Moya said. Her face had hardened as if it was made of cement.

I rose from my chair and walked toward the board. I struggled to multiply fractions and my handwriting was crooked because my hands were shaking.

"You got it wrong. Next time you should listen when I teach," Mrs. Moya said.

I wished the teacher wouldn't humiliate me in front of everyone. When I made eye contact with Kwanele, she looked away.

After I sat down, Mrs. Moya called Ntando to the board. Ntando solved the problem without hesitating. Maybe Doreen was right in calling me an idiot.

An hour before school was over Mrs. Moya called me, Doreen, and two other girls playing Cinderella's stepsisters to the front of the class. I shivered despite the warmth as though someone had poured ice-cold water all over me, and I forgot all the words I'd memorized. Doreen stared at me, her eyes blazing as if ready to burn me alive.

" 'Wake up, Cinderella and make us breakfast! You shouldn't sleep all day,' " Doreen said.

" 'I'll make your breakfast...' " I stuttered. Could I ever act in front of a big crowd?

"Busi, continue," Mrs. Moya said.

I recited the first few lines, then I stumbled. Mrs. Moya struck the table with her ruler.

"You didn't practice, did you?" the teacher said.

"I did, ma'am."

"I'll give someone else your role."

I let out a cry. "Please give me another chance. I'll practice harder."

"My mind is made up. You don't take the play seriously."

"Can Thabisa play Cinderella? She's been reading the play and she's a fast learner," I said. I hoped the teacher wouldn't get mad at me for making the suggestion.

When Thabisa gazed at me with a warm smile on her face, I realized I was making the right decision. Hopefully, she would prove to the class that she deserved a major role in the play.

"Okay, let's see what she can do. Thabisa, do you want to be Cinderella?" Mrs. Moya said.

I sighed because the teacher had taken my suggestion.

"I do, ma'am," Thabisa said.

"Don't waste my time," Mrs. Moya said.

" 'I'll just stay here and imagine what it's like to dance with a handsome prince while you go to the ball,' " Thabisa said after she walked to the front of the room. She didn't stumble as she did during the audition.

" 'You *are* staying here. You must do as you're told or else you'll scrub floors all night long,' " Doreen said, emphasizing each word she spoke.

" 'Yes, ma'am. How could I possibly imagine what it's like to dance with him anyway?' "

As Doreen and Thabisa rehearsed, I wondered how Thabisa had memorized all the words in a few days. I decided offering her the role was a great idea. Thabisa had cheered when the teacher chose me to play Cinderella after the auditions earlier that term. Mrs. Moya applauded and the class fell silent. Everyone's eyes opened wide. Thabisa had surprised them all.

"Hey, you," Doreen called out to me after school. "You couldn't even recite your lines. You are an idiot! I learned my lines within an hour."

"I did the best I could. At least Thabisa and I came up with a great idea."

"I'm glad you're not playing Cinderella anymore. You won't get all the fame."

"I don't want fame, Doreen. I'm happy being me." I turned away and joined Thabisa.

Thabisa and I didn't talk about the play on the way home and neither of us mentioned that I was no longer Cinderella.

"How was the rehearsal?" Grandma asked right away.

"Okay," I said.

"You answer with just one word. Is something the matter?"

"Thabisa is now going to play Cinderella."

"Are you happy?"

I smiled and nodded. At least Grandma didn't ask me to explain why I no longer had the role. "Yes." I felt a mixture of joy and regret.

"I see you are upset about something else," Grandma said.

"I'm okay, Grandma," I said.

Grandma didn't pursue the subject any further.

Minutes later, while I was in my room, I heard a knock and opened the door. It was MaSibanda.

"Thabisa told me that you gave up playing Cinderella for her," MaSibanda said. "She didn't tell me why. Thank you for letting her play Cinderella. She's always liked acting. I hope you have no regrets."

I smiled at MaSibanda, but I didn't tell her I'd actually lost the role. "I'm glad she likes the part."

"I'll be there to watch the play. I'll bring your grandmother, too."

After MaSibanda left, I looked at the time. It was only eight p.m., but I felt tired from lack of sleep, and slipped into bed without playing my music box. Although I was no longer playing Cinderella, I smiled because Thabisa had the role instead of one of the other girls in our class.

Chapter 17

During the weekend, while I sat outside in the shade with Grandma, Thabisa, and MaSibanda, a car pulled up near the house and a man stepped out. As he approached the house, MaSibanda clapped a hand over her mouth, and Thabisa gasped. He looked so much like Thabisa that he had to be her father.

"Hi, Martha," the man said to MaSibanda.

"Jonas," MaSibanda stood up.

"You two know each other?" Grandma said.

The man bowed. "I'm her husband."

MaSibanda straightened her skirt. "Not anymore. What are you doing here?"

"I came to apologize for not taking care of my daughter," Thabisa's father said. "I want Thabisa back in my life. Can we talk?"

When he smiled at Thabisa, his eyes lit up. Thabisa stood tall and didn't move.

Her eyes streamed with tears and she shook her head. "It can't be," she said.

"I'd like to have some time alone with Jonas," MaSibanda said. "Maybe we'll take a walk."

"Thank you, Martha," he said.

Thabisa turned her back on her father, and marched to the kitchen, slamming the door behind her. MaSibanda called after her. I couldn't believe that Thabisa, who was self-composed, had broken down in tears! If my dad had arrived I'd have many questions for him, and I'd cry tears of joy instead. I wished Dad would come to see me and apologize for not writing to me for months.

Grandma said, "I will go inside." I helped her to her feet and held her hand as we shuffled to the kitchen.

Thabisa sat at the kitchen table, rubbing her wet cheeks, and sniffling. I put my hand on her shoulder. "Are you okay?" I asked.

"I can't believe he's back. It's been five years," Thabisa said.

"I will let you children talk." Grandma limped to her bedroom and shut the door.

For the first time, Thabisa had cried before me and I didn't know how to comfort her. I pulled a chair next to her, trying to think of the right words to say. She stopped sniffling, then she looked at me, and tried to smile.

"I was very surprised to see my father. I don't know whether to be happy or sad." Thabisa leaned forward and rested her elbows on the table. "It's too late now. He can't take me away."

"You're not going anywhere. Maybe you should talk to him. He seems to care about you."

"How could you know?"

"I could tell by the look on his face," I said. "He

found you. He must have cared enough to look for you."

"But why now? Why not years ago?"

I didn't answer, not knowing what to say next. Although Dad seemed to be neglecting me too, we had communicated a few months ago.

"Would you like to read the play?" I said, hoping to distract Thabisa.

"Okay."

I went to my room to get *Cinderella*. When I returned to the kitchen, Thabisa's eyes were dry.

" 'Wake up, Cinderella and make us some breakfast. You shouldn't sleep all day!' " I said after sitting down and opening the book.

" 'I'll make your breakfast right away, ma'am. What would you like to eat?' " Thabisa read a Cinderella line from the play.

" 'You should know my favorite meals by now. Now hurry to the kitchen.' " We recited the lines without looking, and I remembered them, not feeling the same pressure I did when I had to learn Cinderella's lines.

"You could very well be Cinderella's stepmother. You're good," Thabisa said.

I smiled. "I'm learning from you."

Grandma reappeared from her room. MaSibanda returned, her eyes gleaming.

"You girls were talking, so I couldn't sleep," Grandma said and turned to MaSibanda. "Where is

Thabisa's father?"

"He's outside," MaSibanda said.

"He should come inside." Grandma sank into a chair next to Thabisa.

MaSibanda stepped outside and returned with Thabisa's father. After everyone sat down, Grandma asked me to serve food to Thabisa's father, but MaSibanda offered to wait on him.

When he finished eating, Grandma and I left so Thabisa and her parents could talk. In my room, I played the music box and dusted the furniture with a rag. Since MaSibanda moved in, I did less housework, but I insisted on cleaning my own room.

As I thought about my father's absence in my daily life, I frowned. Would Thabisa realize how lucky she was to finally have her father back in her life? Today Thabisa had both her parents with her. Time moved slowly while I waited for them to finish talking. I couldn't remember when I last spent time with both my parents. Nowadays I only daydreamed about them chatting without arguing.

After I finished tidying my room, Thabisa burst in without knocking.

"My father is in the sitting room with my mother," Thabisa said. "He and I talked." She sat on my bed and covered her face with her hands. "He wants to take me away. He wants me to transfer to another school in his neighborhood right away. But my brothers will stay in the country."

"That can't happen," I said, sniffling. "You just transferred to Phezulu. Besides, I'd miss you."

Thabisa started sobbing. "I don't want to leave Phezulu. My father says he's sorry for not being with me all this time. I can forgive him for that, but I don't want him to take me away. I like being your friend."

"What does your mother think?" I wound an arm around Thabisa's shoulders.

"She agreed. I should be angry with her, but I'm not. She's had a difficult time taking care of me on her own. We could only afford so little."

I patted Thabisa's arm. "Listen to me. I won't let anyone take you away. Here's what I suggest you do. Talk to your father again. Tell him exactly how you feel about leaving. Make him listen to you. Don't give up."

She nodded. "I'll talk to him again. I agreed to visit him every weekend. You can come with me sometimes." She stood up. "Come and talk to my father. I will talk to him about staying with you later when I'm alone with him."

When we reached the sitting room, Thabisa's parents were laughing and chatting. I sat on a chair next to Grandma and Thabisa sat on the sofa with her parents.

"Thabisa told me about your play and that you offered her your role." Thabisa's father smiled as he spoke to me. "You're a nice girl."

I smiled but didn't answer.

We talked more about the play. After Thabisa's father left, MaSibanda bustled in the kitchen, dusting shelves and polishing the floor. She appeared to have even more energy than usual.

That night, Mama called to find out how I was doing.

"How is Dad?"

"He's fine. I told him you were thinking about him."

"I feel a bit sad because Thabisa's father visited her today and Dad hasn't. Her father wants to take her away. I don't want to lose her too like I've lost touch with Florence."

"I told your father to write to you. I know it must be difficult to hear that your friend might be going away, but remember you can always visit each other."

"I know, Mama. I will miss her even though she's not leaving the country like Florence."

After I hung up the phone, I stayed awake in bed, thinking about the day's events. I was close to losing another friend. The song, "Forever Your Friend," played in my head.

Chapter 18

A week before the play, Mrs. Moya told me to bring the clothes I wanted to lend my classmates and my music box to school. The class would rehearse again. When I returned home, I packed my clothes in a small suitcase. Before I put my music box inside the suitcase, I stroked it gently as if it were a cat. "You mean so much to me. I hope you bring me good luck one of these days," I whispered.

The following day, I showed the music box to Mrs. Moya in class after all my classmates had arrived.

"It's lovely and perfect for the play," Mrs. Moya said. "Where did you buy it?"

My lips curved into a broad smile. "My friend Florence gave it to me before she left for South Africa. It means a lot to me."

Doreen grumbled, but I continued to smile.

"What's the matter, Doreen?" Mrs. Moya said. "I won't tolerate rude behavior. Do you want to leave the classroom right now?"

"No, ma'am," Doreen said.

Later, I went to the bathroom with some of the girls in my class so they could try on the clothes I lent them for the play. When Doreen tried on one of the dresses, the sleeves ripped.

"Look what you did," I said.

"Sorry," she said, laughing. When she pulled off the dress, the sleeves ripped even more.

I snatched the dress from her. "This should stop!"

"Too bad."

This time I wouldn't let Doreen get away with ruining something of mine. Without saying another word, I headed to the classroom, where Mrs. Moya was seated and told her what Doreen did to my dress. How could I continue to be calm when Doreen was obviously taking advantage of me? She clearly had no intention of changing her attitude.

"I'll have a word with Doreen when she returns to class," Mrs. Moya said.

As soon as Doreen walked into the classroom with the rest of my classmates, Mrs. Moya called her to her table.

"Why did you rip Busi's dress?" Mrs. Moya asked Doreen.

"It was an accident, ma'am," Doreen said in a low voice.

"Did you apologize?" Mrs. Moya asked. Before Doreen could answer, the teacher continued. "You'll have detention on Thursday. If you do anything foolish again, you won't act in the play. Do you understand?"

"I didn't mean—"

"You heard me. Now go and rehearse," Mrs. Moya said.

Doreen glared at me before sitting at her desk. I straightened my back and stared back at her, trying not to show any emotion. Although I believed she would seek revenge, I was glad I'd told the teacher about my dress. I wished Doreen would lose her role right away. When Doreen ruined my library book, Mrs. Moya had already warned her that she could lose her role.

A few minutes later, I sat on the grass watching the final rehearsal. Since I no longer had any lines to practice, I didn't have to rehearse. Doreen forgot some of her lines, and she yelled so loud that Mrs. Moya scolded her.

After Mrs. Moya told the class to take a break, Thabisa told me that she was going to the bathroom. Vumani joined me.

"I'm sorry you won't be playing Cinderella," he said. "I think you deserved the role."

I looked at him and smiled. "Thanks. I *am* glad Thabisa is playing Cinderella."

"She does perform well. Are you having a good term so far?"

"There were times I wished some of our classmates would be nicer, but I'm happy now. I have a good friend."

"You know what?" Vumani said. "In fifth grade, I felt I didn't have real friends. The boys just wanted to use me because they thought I was smart. When I stopped helping them with homework, they turned against me. They came around after they found out I'm a good athlete. I still wonder if some of them just like me for my skills."

"I can't imagine anyone not liking you. You're so friendly."

Vumani shrugged. "I should have spoken to you sooner. Don't let anyone try to put you down." He walked toward his friends.

After listening to Vumani, my spirits soared.

Fifteen minutes later, Mrs. Moya called the class to resume the rehearsal, but she kept it shorter than the actual play. Instead of glass slippers, Thabisa wore my old pair of silver shoes. When she danced with Vumani, she constantly stepped on his toes, and some of the students giggled. He gave the music box to Thabisa, and then I took it and packed it in my backpack right away.

Mrs. Moya let the class go home early so Thabisa and I decided to go to a store to buy cokes. There Doreen and Ntando were talking to classmates. They whispered something to their friends and laughed.

"What are you doing here?" Doreen asked, walking toward me. "Shouldn't you be at home practicing your lines?"

"Not now, Doreen."

"Busi doesn't have any lines to practice. She's not

118

good enough to be Cinderella." Ntando faked a cry. She and her friends laughed and customers turned to look at them.

"Can we go home now?" Thabisa said to me.

"Let's buy our drinks first," I said and pulled money from my bag.

"Your friend is a clown. She can't even dance," Doreen said to me. "You saw the way she was stepping on Vumani's feet."

"She danced very well." I breathed in and out, trying to stay calm.

"Are you still looking forward to the play?" Doreen asked. "You don't want to disappoint your grandmother."

"Why do you say so?" I folded my arms.

"The play won't take place as planned. I have detention because of you," Doreen said. She pulled Ntando's hand and together they strutted out of the store before I could say anything else.

What could Doreen and Ntando possibly have planned? Apparently, Doreen never changed her mind about ruining the play. I had been right all along when I thought she was out to get me. When I saw her tomorrow, I'd talk to her again. I had to make her realize that trying to stop the play from taking place was a mistake.

The evening before the play, the phone rang and I rushed to answer it, hoping it was Mama, but it was Thabisa's father. I handed the phone to Thabisa and left the sitting room to give her privacy.

After Thabisa finished talking to her father, she told me he was arriving the next morning. The play would be held in the afternoon.

"I begged my father again to let me stay at Phezulu but he didn't listen to me," Thabisa said.

My heart sank. "I'm so sorry."

"What am I going to do?"

"I'll talk to your mother," I said, rubbing my eyes. "She's been with you all your life so it would be hard for her to let you go. I'm sure if I talk to her she'll persuade your father to let you stay."

Thabisa shook her head. "Thanks, Busi. But you can't solve all my problems."

"Why don't you let me try?"

"By the way, my father bought me a gown to wear for the play, so you don't have to lend me one," Thabisa said.

"That's nice," I said. I'd hoped I could give Thabisa some of my clothes, but now that her father was back in her life, she might not accept hand-me-downs. As if Thabisa really was Cinderella, she was being transformed into a princess who could afford gowns.

"He says he saw news about the play in the local newspaper," Thabisa said.

"Fantastic. The play will be popular."

Mrs. Sibanda shook her head when I explained that Thabisa wanted to stay in Phezulu.

"You've helped us enough. It's time for us to move on. I'm sorry, Busi."

"But she has friends here. She has me." My eyes filled with tears.

"It's been difficult trying to make ends meet," Mrs. Sibanda said. "I will stay with you and Grandma. I'm thinking about what's best for Thabisa right now. I'll make sure she visits often and she'll go with you on your school trip in April."

I wished I'd asked Grandma to talk to MaSibanda instead and I was afraid I'd lose another friend. This time I had to make sure I kept in touch with Thabisa.

When I awoke the next morning, my stomach growled. I went to the kitchen before bathing and filled a kettle with water for tea and set in on the stove. From the cupboard, I pulled out cups and saucers and tea leaves, and then I made some toast. While I was eating, Grandma entered the room still wearing her nightgown and a headdress she wore to bed.

"You're up early." Grandma leaned her cane against the table and sat next to me. "Did you sleep well?"

"Yes, Grandma. I'm excited about the play."

"I am glad I'll watch your play. I told you I wouldn't miss it."

I sipped my tea. "I'm also glad you'll be there. You're not disappointed in me, are you?"

"How can you say that?"

"I'm not playing Cinderella," I said. "Mrs. Moya wanted to choose someone else because I couldn't memorize my lines. I did suggest Thabisa play Cinderella though."

Grandma took my hand in hers. "I am sorry, Grandchild. You had enough worries. You're good and brave. I am very proud of you."

I smiled. "Thank you."

But when I remembered my confrontation with Doreen and Ntando the day before, I started to worry about what the two girls had planned for the day. I needed to arrive at school early so I could have a word with them. My class had to arrive at school by noon and I planned to be there earlier.

I scrambled some eggs for Grandma and made her a cup of tea. Afterwards, I bathed and changed. The clothes I was going to wear for the play were at school where *Cinderella* would take place that Saturday, but I was taking the music box with me.

When I arrived at school, Mrs. Moya and a few other classmates were already in the classroom.

"Start putting out chairs, desks, and tables," Mrs. Moya said. "Take them from different classrooms."

After I gave the music box to the teacher, I helped my classmates carry tables and desks outside. Kwanele and Bongi were struggling to carry the teacher's table, so I rushed to help them lift it.

"It looks like you could use some help." I smiled at them.

"We sure could use more help," Kwanele said.

"Good luck playing the fairy godmother," I said.

Kwanele grinned. "Thanks. It's going to be so much fun."

As more students arrived, they joined me and those who were already there. We all carried chairs from classrooms for spectators to sit on. I chatted with Vumani and the other girls in my classroom. I smiled all the time.

Thabisa arrived carrying her cream gown, which looked like a wedding dress and even had a train. Everyone was too busy to comment. The dress was lovelier than the one I had wanted to lend her.

Together with my classmates, I spread a faded carpet on the ground to set the stage and put three chairs and a table on the stage for Cinderella's stepmother and stepsisters. Cinderella would sit on the floor and lie on a tattered blanket, covered by a worn out sheet. Some of the families in the neighborhood had contributed the blanket, sheet, and clothes for the rest of the students who'd be in the play. After we finished setting up the stage, my classmates went to the bathroom to change into their costumes. Then everyone returned to the classroom.

"Those of you who don't have any lines to recite can sell tickets," Mrs. Moya said. "I'll be supervising you. You'll sell the tickets at the school gate. Be sure to count money carefully and give the correct change. Also, be courteous to everyone."

At one p.m. Doreen and Ntando still hadn't arrived, and my heart started pounding. Mrs. Moya
paced the room, constantly looking at her watch. Fifteen minutes before the play, Doreen wasn't there. I
clenched my hands and clamped my teeth. I felt
ready to explode and yell at our teacher for giving
an important role to Doreen. My eyes met Mrs.
Moya's, but I looked away, not wanting her to notice
my anger.

Chapter 19

I looked outside. I squinted as the sunlight streamed through the window. People had already started buying tickets and were settling into chairs, waiting for the play to begin. Even the first and second-grade chairs were lined up for the audience to sit on. Some of the women wore sunhats and bright dresses while the man wore button-down shirts. Doreen hadn't arrived and I concluded that she had planned to miss the play after all.

"It's almost time for the play and Doreen isn't here. We might have to cancel it," Mrs. Moya said, folding her arms. She now sat at her table.

I could hear my heart hammering. I had to think of something fast.

"But they already bought tickets. We can't tell them there won't be a play. We worked so hard for this play. We can't give up."

"We'll reimburse those who already bought tickets."

"I can play Cinderella's stepmother, ma'am," I said. "I know some of her lines and I can make up the parts I don't know."

Mrs. Moya uncrossed her arms. "Are you sure? I don't want the play to be a disaster."

"I'll do my best, ma'am."

"But you couldn't even recite Cinderella's lines."

"Mrs. Moya, Busi and I have been reading the play together. She knows her lines," Thabisa said.

"All right, you can play the stepmother, Busi."

"Thank you, ma'am." I smiled at the teacher. "I'll do my best. No one will know that I didn't have the role all along."

Two minutes before the play began, Ntando marched into the classroom, panting as if she'd run all the way to school. Instead of shouting at Ntando, Mrs. Moya stared at her long and hard.

"You cannot be part of the play. You should have been here over an hour ago," Mrs. Moya said. She turned her attention to the class. "I want the play to be successful. You must speak clearly, so everyone can understand you. Stay in the classroom until it's your turn to go on stage. Let's get going. We're already running late."

Outside Grandma and MaSibanda sat in the front row. I waved to them and smiled. Would I remember Cinderella's stepmother's lines? I didn't want to look like a fool again.

"I didn't see my father, did you?" Thabisa said just before she and I entered the stage.

I shook my head. "He's probably sitting in the back somewhere."

The play began and the audience fell silent, but

my heart continued to beat fast. In the first act, Thabisa lay on the stage, covered with a tattered sheet. I entered the stage, pulled back the sheet, and read my lines. After Thabisa read hers, the girls playing Cinderella's stepsisters entered the stage.

" 'Cinderella, you didn't iron any clothes for me to wear. I have to wear these wrinkled ones!' " the older stepsister said.

" 'Why don't you go to my room and make my bed right away?' " the younger stepsister said.

" 'What about breakfast?' "

" 'Didn't I tell you not to ask questions?' " I said. " 'Cook our breakfast right away. You should have cleaned our rooms already!' "

" 'I didn't want to disturb you while you were sleeping.' "

" 'Hush! You are very stubborn,' " I said " 'Move fast, you have a lot to do.' "

When my eyes landed on Grandma, she waved her paper fan and smiled. I nodded. Regardless of how the rest of the year turned out, I would always remember this day. Now that I was playing a more prominent role, Grandma would get to see me more throughout the play. I gained confidence and relaxed. I was amazed at how easily words came to me. Thabisa's father sat behind MaSibanda. Thabisa had seen him too because she was smiling. The thought of Thabisa leaving Phezulu made me frown. But maybe she loved her father too much to lose him again. The reunion was a good thing.

After the first act, the crowd applauded and my class took a break.

"You're doing very well, Busi," Thabisa said after we returned to our classroom.

"You too! If it wasn't for you, I would never have practiced the stepmother's lines."

Mrs. Moya entered the classroom, smiling. "Good job, Thabisa," she said. "You too, Busi. I'm impressed. You're playing the stepmother very well."

"Thank you, ma'am," Thabisa and I said at the same time. I grinned. Mrs. Moya had given me a compliment so I must be doing something right.

"May I sit with the audience to watch Thabisa until it's my turn to go on stage again?"

"You may," Mrs. Moya said. "Just don't get so excited that you forget the rest of your lines."

Ten minutes later, I sat next to Grandma and Thabisa started acting again.

" 'I wish I could go to the ball, but I don't have any nice clothes. Why would the prince choose to dance with me?' "

" 'I can make all your wishes come true, Cinderella,' " Kwanele said. " 'You will go to the ball. Just listen to everything I tell you to do.' "

Toward the end of the play, Vumani gave Thabisa the music box. She held the music box to

128

her chest as the crowd roared.

"Good job," Mrs. Moya said to our class after we returned to our classroom. "Many people paid to watch the play so I'm sure we have enough money for the trip."

My classmates and I cheered.

"Sorry, I have to go now. I got an emergency call. My daughter is not well," Mrs. Moya said. "Before you leave, clean up and return all the tables and chairs to the classrooms. See you next week."

Back in the bathroom, I grinned and plopped my backpack on the floor, and then I changed my clothes. Now I could join Grandma.

Chapter 20

Thabisa and I found Grandma, MaSibanda, and Thabisa's father waiting outside. We all bought food in the cafeteria and sat outside at a table located in the shade.

"You girls did very well. I am proud." Grandma leaned her cane on the table.

"Thank you, Grandma," I said.

Thabisa's father's eyes shifted to Thabisa and he smiled. "I'm very proud of you, my daughter."

Thabisa smiled back. "Thanks, Dad. I'm glad you could make it."

I glanced to my right. Doreen sat next to Ntando at a table. Why did Doreen arrive after the play had ended? When our eyes met, Doreen glared at me, but I just pursed my lips and looked away.

"Do you see Doreen?" I said to Thabisa, pointing toward Doreen and Ntando. "I can't believe she's here now."

Thabisa tilted her head. "I see her. Let's just ignore her and have fun. We're having a good day."

"MaSibanda took pictures of the play," Grandma said.

"Wow! I can't wait to see them," I said. Mama would love to see them too.

"Me too," Thabisa said.

After we finished eating, Thabisa and I walked to our classroom. Most of my clothes lay piled on a table, and only a few were folded. Vumani and a few of my classmates were rearranging chairs and desks.

"You saved the day, Busi," he said.

"Thanks. You played the prince very well." I remembered that I hadn't asked for my music box back after the play was over. "Did you see my music box?" I asked.

Vumani pointed to the table. "I put it on the table with all your clothes."

I walked toward the table to look for the music box. When I didn't see it, I searched through my clothes, but the music box wasn't there.

"I can't find my music box. When did you put it on the table?" I asked Vumani, my heart pounding hard.

"Soon after the play, Kwanele and I asked everyone for your dresses, and I made sure I put everything together with the music box," Vumani said. "I'm sorry. I should have given it to you."

"It's not your fault," I said, my voice quavering. Eager to talk to Grandma about the play, I had hurried to her, forgetting about my music box. Why didn't I think of it sooner?

"We'll help you look for it," Thabisa said.

We searched through the clothes again and under desks and chairs, but we couldn't find the music box.

My hands trembled as I shoved my dresses in a plastic bag. The music box was still missing even after we cleared the table. *Someone must have stolen it.* Sweat trickled down my face as I looked through the clothes I'd already put in the bag.

I turned to girls from my class who stood in a circle. "Have you seen my music box?" My lips shook slightly.

The girls shook their heads at the same time and I couldn't read their facial expressions. My eyes watered even though I was trying hard to be brave. What would happen if the music box disappeared forever? Had Doreen and Ntando stolen it? Neither of them had helped clear the stage after the play was over and Doreen hadn't shown up for the play at all. How could I enjoy the school trip now? I'd hoped I could make more friends if I traveled somewhere with my classmates.

I wiped my eyes and stopped crying, then I helped my classmates carry chairs back to the classrooms.

"I really hope you find the music box today," Thabisa said.

I sniffled. "I might never find it. I can't believe what has happened."

Did I deserve the gift Florence gave me? What would she think if she heard the news?

Following Mrs. Moya's orders, my class picked up trash and cleaned the yard. Together with Thabisa and Vumani, I searched the schoolyard for the music box, but we didn't find it. Shoulders drooping, I finally gave up on the search and Thabisa and I headed to Thabisa's father's car.

Chapter 21

"You look sad. What is the matter?" Grandma said to me at home that day after Thabisa's father left. "You were very quiet in the car." We sat at the kitchen table drinking water while Thabisa was in her room with MaSibanda.

"My music box is missing," I said through tears. I explained how I'd lent it to my classmates for the play.

"You will find it. You were kind to lend them something so precious," Grandma said.

The next day, I didn't accompany Thabisa to lunch with her father. I couldn't believe that the music box had vanished. If only I'd been more careful and kept a close eye on it. In my room, I flung my dresses in the hamper, sprawled on my bed, and buried my face in my pillow. I cried hard.

I had to find out for sure whether Doreen and Ntando had stolen my music box. After I lay down for what seemed like hours, I rolled off the bed, slipped on my shoes, and headed to the kitchen. I found Grandma and MaSibanda chatting.

"I keep thinking that I may never see my music box again," I said. "If Ntando and Doreen did steal it, they won't be foolish enough to bring it to school."

Grandma took my hand. "Your teacher will help you."

"I hope she can." I squeezed Grandma's hand. "I've known that Doreen and Ntando wanted to ruin the trip for a while now. That makes me think they would try to steal."

"We'll do everything we can to find your music box. We'll ask the neighbors, if necessary," MaSibanda said.

I sighed. Grandma and MaSibanda were optimistic, but I was already losing hope.

An hour later, while I sat in the sitting room playing solitaire, Thabisa entered the room, dressed in a blue dress with ruffles, and carrying a black purse.

"Wow. Your dress is lovely." I smiled. "How was lunch?"

"Great. I really enjoyed my father's company. But I kept wishing you were there." Thabisa sat next to me and clasped her hands. Her fingernails were trimmed and her hands shone with Vaseline.

"Sorry, I didn't come." My smile turned into a frown. "I've been thinking about my music box and don't have an appetite."

"I know that Phezulu Primary is not the best place on earth," Thabisa said. "But I think things were getting better."

"You're right. I thought it was getting better until my music box was stolen." I nodded. "I'll keep my head up, but I'll talk to Doreen first thing on Monday. I want some answers."

"Tell Mrs. Moya about the music box first. She'll know what to do."

"That's what Grandma says. But how can I keep quiet when I see Doreen and Ntando?"

"Just try. I know it won't be easy."

I smiled, but I knew the smile didn't reach my eyes.

The weekend dragged for me. The following Monday morning, I walked to school early without Thabisa. When I arrived, Mrs. Moya was the only one in class. I told her about the music box.

Mrs. Moya shook her head. "I'll make the culprit confess."

After the rest of my classmates filed into the classroom and settled in their seats, Mrs. Moya told all of us that we'd raised enough money to go to Matopos. Everyone cheered.

Mrs. Moya continued, "Busi's music box is missing and I believe that one of you is responsible. The trip is postponed until it's found." She turned to Doreen. "Come to the front of the classroom, right now."

Doreen shuffled towards the teacher, her shoulders drooping.

"You have detention again next Wednesday for not showing up on the day of the play. You won't go on the school trip." The teacher scolded Doreen, who nodded, then returned to her seat.

The class fell silent and I only heard the shuffling of feet. I turned around to face Doreen, but she avoided eye contact. She stared at Mrs. Moya, her mouth slightly open. I wished Doreen's punishment had been worse. Ntando's head was tilted toward the window and she didn't seem to be paying attention to Mrs. Moya.

"Whoever has Busi's music box must confess or face suspension. I mean every word I say," Mrs. Moya said, pacing the room. "I'll search everyone's bag."

None of my classmates raised their hands, and they kept quiet. Mrs. Moya searched everyone's bag, but no one had the music box. Did Mrs. Moya think that someone was foolish enough to carry the music box around?

After the bell rang, my classmates chatted among themselves.

"I will be very disappointed if we don't go on this trip," Kwanele said. "Whoever stole the music box should be thrown out of school."

"Busi probably hid it to get one of us in trouble," Doreen said.

"I doubt it. She's not bad really," Kwanele said. "She did a good job playing the stepmother. I wish..."

The students continued talking and I listened without saying anything. Maybe once I proved that Doreen and Ntando were the culprits, I'd finally have my classmates on my side.

After everyone left, I asked Mrs. Moya if we could still go to Matopos even if no one owned up, but she was adamant.

"I will donate the money to the school unless we find your music box. I know you can afford to go to Matopos on your own if you like, but I'll punish everyone else," Mrs. Moya said. I didn't pursue the topic, but marched out of the classroom and joined Thabisa who was waiting outside. Doreen had already left for the day so I didn't get a chance to talk to her alone.

Thabisa and I were silent as we plodded down the street, our shoes rapping the tarred road. I clung to my backpack as if I were afraid someone would snatch it from me. When I reached home, I stomped on the rug outside my house to remove the dust on my shoes and followed Thabisa into the house.

Chapter 22

"I told Mrs. Moya about my music box," I said to Grandma after greeting her.

She sat at the kitchen table, folding dishtowels with MaSibanda.

"You will get it back. This is a small town," Grandma said. "Can you go to the store to buy milk after eating?" She fumbled in her shirt pocket and pulled out some bills. "Here is the money. Don't worry about anything."

"I'll go as soon as I change clothes. I'm not hungry," I said. I'd packed a big lunch that day after having a light breakfast.

"I'm not hungry either," Thabisa said. "I'll go with Busi."

Later we walked to the store. Few people were there and the shelves were loaded with bread, tea leaves, sweets, bags of cornmeal, and other foods. We waited in line.

After we bought the milk, I spotted Doreen walking out of the store, a plastic bag in hand, and hurried after her.

"What are you doing here?" Doreen asked.

"Shopping, what about you?" I said, my hands on my hips.

Doreen folded her arms. "What do you think I'd be doing in a grocery store?"

"What were you doing the day of the play? You showed up after it was all over."

"So what if I did?"

"My music box is missing."

"Why are you telling me that? I don't care. Now get out of my way." Doreen brushed against me, lifted her plastic bag over her shoulder, and hurried toward the door.

I hurried after her. "If you give me my music box back, I won't tell Mrs. Moya that you took it." I was being bold since I didn't have proof that Doreen stole the music box.

Doreen threw her head back. "How dare you accuse me of stealing! Of course, I don't have your music box." She took a step closer to me.

I straightened my shoulders and looked Doreen in the eyes. "You had the opportunity to steal, Doreen. I know you're trying hard to make me miserable. I won't let you."

Doreen seemed at a loss for words. She stared at me hard and for a second I thought she was going to smack me, instead, she turned away muttering, "If you follow me, I'll make you wish you weren't born."

"Are you really sure she has the music box?" Thabisa said after Doreen left.

I nodded. "We should think of a plan to get it back."

"What should we do?"

"Search her room?"

"How? We can't break into her house and I don't think she'll let us in."

"We'll think of something," I said. "Ntando is probably involved, and maybe they planned to steal the music box together."

"That's very likely."

When we returned home, I put the milk in the refrigerator and gave Grandma her change. Afterwards, Thabisa and I did our homework in the kitchen while Grandma slept in her room, and MaSibanda swept the yard. Instead of asking Thabisa for help with every single math question, I tried to solve most of them on my own. In a few weeks, I'd have examinations and I was determined to pass every subject. As I worked, I tried not to think about my music box.

After I finished the math problems, I compared my answers with Thabisa's, and only two of them were different. We worked on the problems together and Thabisa's answers were all correct, but I smiled.

"I can't believe I only got two questions wrong," I said. I was making progress. I shut my notebook and laid it on the table. "I usually do poorly in Math."

"You *are* a good student and you work hard too."

"I didn't work hard enough before. I learned it from you," I said. "Grandma and Mama will be so proud if I pass Math."

I was hopeful that my school life would be easier as the year progressed. Since I helped my classmates set up the stage for the school play, overall, they were nicer to me, and Vumani talked to me more often now. As long as Doreen wasn't around me, school life was tolerable.

"I think I'll do better than Ntando this time. Last year she beat me in every subject but Ndebele," I said. "She'd probably say, 'Don't get a big head now. You are still dumb anyway,' " I imitated Ntando's voice.

"Wow, you sound just like Ntando!" Thabisa said.

"I *was* trying to talk like her," I said. "Maybe I could trick Doreen into thinking I'm Ntando?"

"How are you going to do that?"

"I'll call Doreen pretending to be Ntando," I said. "I've heard Ntando talking about calling her, so she must have a phone at least. I'll just ask her about the music box. Doreen will admit she has it if she thinks I'm Ntando. If we can prove she stole the music box, she'll have no choice but to own up."

"I like your idea. I think you can do it. You're good at acting. Your voice sounded different when you tried out for Cinderella."

I hoped my plan would work. But even if Thabisa and I found out for sure that Doreen had the music box, Mrs. Moya might not take our word. Someone else needed to hear Doreen confess.

"I hope she'll feel guilty if she stole the music

box," Thabisa said.

"I can't imagine Doreen feeling guilty about anything. She ruined my library book," I said. "We need a witness when she admits she has my music box, but I can't involve Grandma. She might not like the idea."

That night, while I lay in bed, I wondered if my plan would work, but I couldn't think of anything else I could do to make Doreen and Ntando confess. The girls hadn't responded when Mrs. Moya told the class that the thief could be suspended from school. I shut my eyes, trying to fall asleep, but I couldn't help thinking about the music box. My nighttime routine was disrupted since I couldn't play "Forever Your Friend." After what seemed like several hours, I started dozing. I turned to my side and covered my head with my sheet.

The next day in school, Mrs. Moya asked if anyone wanted to show the rest of the class how to solve another math problem similar to the one she'd assigned the day before. No one volunteered.

"Busi, why don't you go to the board?" Mrs. Moya asked.

I stood up and faced my classmates before going to the front of the class. A few students gave me blank stares and some bit their fingernails. But no one groaned.

When I wrote on the board, my hands started shaking. I remembered how I'd solved yesterday's assignments and worked on the fractions faster than I normally did. When I finished, I faced Mrs. Moya.

"Good job, Busi," Mrs. Moya said. "You got it right in no time at all."

I beamed as I walked back to my seat. A few of my classmates smiled. Maybe Phezulu Primary would be a better place.

During lunch break, Thabisa and I watched Vumani and his friends kicking a ball.

"Would you like to play ball with us?" Vumani asked.

"Sure." I smiled.

Thabisa nodded. "That would be awesome."

I quickly finished my cheese sandwich and apple juice and rose to my feet to join the boys. Thabisa was already chatting with them. We played on the grass using tall sticks as goals, kicking the ball to one another, laughing and cheering. Two boys who were goalkeepers stood across from each other, ready to kick the ball.

Should I ask Vumani to help me get my music box back? He was the only boy I liked in my class. When we stopped playing, I shared my idea with Thabisa.

"I was thinking the same thing. We should ask him," Thabisa said.

I called Vumani and he walked over to us without his friends.

"Would you do us a favor?" I said.

"It depends on what you want me to do."

"My music box is still missing and I believe that Doreen stole it," I said. "I'm going to call her and pretend to be Ntando. We want you to hear Doreen admit she has the music box."

Vumani sighed. "That's a serious accusation. Why do you need me to be there?"

"You can be our witness in case we need to talk to the teacher," I said. "She might not believe me and Thabisa alone because we're close friends."

"Are you using a speakerphone?" Vumani asked.

I didn't have a speakerphone. How was Vumani going to know what Doreen was saying on the phone?

"We didn't think of that," I said.

Vumani rubbed his temples, staring ahead as if deep in thought.

"I'll help you," Vumani said. "Actually my parents know Doreen's family so I can easily find her number. My dad has a cell phone he lets me borrow sometimes. He'll be home this afternoon. We can put it on loudspeaker and use it to make the call. That way we'll all be able to hear what Doreen is saying."

"I like your idea, Vumani," I said. "We could stay in school later to talk to Doreen after she gets home. Please look up her number."

"I'll go home as soon as classes are over, and return with the cell phone," Vumani said.

The rest of the day went slowly for me and I thought about the plan in class. Would everything work out? Doreen hurried out of the classroom as soon as the afternoon bell rang. Vumani also headed home. Thabisa and I were the last students to leave the classroom. We waited for Vumani at the school gate as we had planned.

Hours seemed to pass while we waited. We grew tired of standing, so we sat on a bench close to the gate where we would see Vumani coming. More students left the school and soon Thabisa and I seemed to be the only ones there.

"I wonder what's taking Vumani so long." I shifted in my seat. I was losing patience and I felt thirsty.

"I'm sure he'll come eventually."

"What if he changed his mind?"

"There he is." Thabisa pointed at Vumani.

"Oh, good!" I sighed. We stood up and headed towards him.

"Sorry, it took me so long." Vumani's pocket bulged. "My father wasn't home so I had to wait for him. I have the cell phone."

I smiled. "That's great. Now we can make our call."

Vumani dug the cell phone and a paper out of his pocket. "Here it is and the phone number too."

I cleared my throat. "I hope I do sound like Ntando. Let's hope Doreen answers the phone."

Chapter 23

I held my breath as Vumani put the cell phone on loudspeaker and increased the volume.

"Hi, it's Ntando," I said.

"Hi. Where are you? You sound a little different," Doreen said.

"At school—. I'm home. Do you have the music box in your room?"

"Of course. We hid it together, remember," Doreen said. "Busi will never see it again. I plan to sell it."

I paused.

"Ntando, are you there?" Doreen asked.

I gripped the phone. "Doreen. This is not Ntando. It's Busi. We know you have the music box. You must own up." My voice was back to normal.

"You tricked me! I thought I was talking to Ntando. How could you?"

"Doreen, we're using a cell phone on loudspeaker and we heard the conversation," Vumani said. "All my friends are here, so you can't hide. Soon everyone else will know you're a thief. Give Busi her music box back."

Doreen hung up. What if she still refused to own up? Would Mrs. Moya believe us? I thought she liked

Vumani because he was a good student. Hopefully, she would believe him.

"Thank you, Vumani, for your help," I said. "And you too, Thabisa. We'll just have to wait to see what Doreen does for now."

Thabisa smiled. "You're welcome. I didn't do much really."

"Oh, yes you did!"

"I'm glad I could help," Vumani said. "There are things I know about Doreen that most people don't. She has an older sister who's smart and thinks she's better than Doreen. I think Doreen's sister is just as bad as Doreen, but her family supports her. She likes to put others down including Doreen."

"Do you think that's why Doreen is so mean? Because her sister is mean to her?" I asked.

Thabisa nodded. "It sounds like Doreen is putting others down because her sister, maybe even her whole family puts her down. Maybe it makes her feel superior to do so."

"Good thinking, Thabisa," Vumani said. "Anyway, I've got to go. See you."

On the way home, I wondered what Doreen would do next. How could she get away now that Vumani had told her all his friends knew she stole the music box?

Doreen wasn't in school the next day, so Thabisa and I decided to go to her house afterwards. We knocked on the door and Doreen answered it.

"What are you doing here?" she asked, her lips quivering.

"Give me back my music box." I held the door, afraid Doreen would shut it.

"I told Ntando what happened and now she's mad at me," Doreen said. "You shouldn't have tricked me."

"Enough is enough, Doreen. You've gone too far. You can't take things that don't belong to you. It's so wrong."

"I don't have your music box."

"Stop being a bully and a thief. You steal from me just because you think you can get away with it. I won't have it."

Doreen folded her arms. "What are you going to do?"

"Soon everyone will know what kind of a person you really are. Do you want to have more detention because of stealing? You've got to realize that they'll be consequences for your actions." I held my head up high. "Mrs. Moya will learn about this very soon. I'm leaving. If you have any sense at all, you'll return what doesn't belong to you."

I turned and walked away, then Doreen yelled. I tilted my head.

"You can have your lousy music box! It's not worth much anyway," Doreen shouted and walked back indoors.

When she returned with the music box, tears

filled my eyes. I examined it and to my relief, it looked as good as it had the day of the play.

"I expect you to confess in class tomorrow."

Doreen's lips shook. "Why should I? I gave you what you asked for."

"You've got to take responsibility for your actions. See you in school," I said to Doreen.

At home, I finally told Grandma that Doreen had returned my music box, and I asked her not to confront Doreen's parents or Mrs. Moya.

"She should be punished for stealing. Tell your teacher what happened," Grandma said.

The next day in school, while Thabisa and I sat with Vumani and his friends during lunch break, Kwanele approached us. We fell silent.

"I'm sorry about your music box," Kwanele said. "I can't believe the rumors that Doreen stole it. That's awful!"

"Thanks, Kwanele!" I said.

"I like your smile, Busi," Kwanele said. "I remember the day you just smiled when Doreen yelled at you. I thought you were so brave."

I grinned. Kwanele had noticed the change in me.

As more students talked to me about Doreen and the music box, I guessed Vumani had told his friends the trick we played on Doreen, and they spread the news. Doreen had returned to school that day, but she sat alone, pulling at the grass.

"I'm going to have a word with Doreen," I said to Thabisa.

When I approached her, Doreen was nibbling on a sandwich.

"Are you going to confess? Everyone now knows what happened."

"What choice do I have?"

"You should mention that Ntando is involved."

Doreen shrugged. "Whatever."

After the bell rang, I approached Mrs. Moya and told her that Doreen had something to say. Everyone stared at Doreen.

"Is there something you want to say, Doreen?"

"I don't know what Busi wants me to say. I returned her music box," Doreen said. Almost all of my classmates booed.

"Be quiet or else everyone will have detention," Mrs. Moya said. "Why did you have the music box?"

"I was going to give it back."

I turned to face Ntando, who'd buried her face on her desk. Before Doreen sat down, Mrs. Moya left the classroom without saying a word, and returned with the headmistress.

"Do you know what happens to children who are thieves?" the headmistress wagged a finger at Doreen, and she walked towards Ntando. "Stand up," she said to Ntando. "You and Doreen are going to have detention every day for the rest the term."

"Do you hear that?" Mrs. Moya said to Doreen

151

and Ntando.

Neither Doreen nor Ntando made eye contact with the teacher as they nodded. None of the other students said anything. The class was silent for the remainder of the lessons. When my eyes met Vumani's, I smiled, and he nodded and smiled back.

After the bell rang, Doreen remained in her seat, sniffling and rubbing her eyes. I actually felt sorry her.

When Thabisa and I returned home, I told Grandma about my day at school and she was sympathetic.

I turned to Thabisa and smiled. "I'm so glad you helped me get my music box back."

Thabisa smiled back. "I'm happy your plan worked."

"Before I forget, you have a package. I put it in your room," Grandma said. "Also, your dad called. He says he wants to visit you in August. He'll call back."

"Yay, that's great! I can't wait to see him."

In my bedroom, I ripped open the package and in it was a CD from Florence with the single, "Forever Your Friend" and the song lyrics. I cheered and played the CD right away. Tears of happiness filled my eyes. I'd finally heard from a friend I'd thought I'd lost. Now I could get in touch with Florence and I'd have another good friend. In her note, Florence apologized for not writing sooner and said she missed me.

As "Forever Your Friend" played, I reminisced about everything that had happened since Florence left. I thought about Thabisa transferring to Phezulu, the *Cinderella* play, Grandma's illness, Mama's arrival, the disappearance of the music box, and finally Doreen's confession. The music box had consoled me on sad days, but it also brought me joy. Just as I'd hoped, it had brought me good luck. After I took my music box to school, my attitude changed as I interacted more with the other students, especially while we were all setting up the stage for the play. They'd also noticed how carefree I was when I responded to Doreen's teasing as the term neared the end and they treated me better.

Thabisa had befriended me after Florence left for South Africa, and she'd stayed with me when Grandma was in the hospital. She was a true friend indeed. I couldn't believe that Thabisa would be leaving Phezulu soon.

I played the music box and decided to give it to Thabisa. Although the music box meant a lot to me, I felt that Thabisa deserved it.

I picked up the music box and sighed, feeling as if I was making the biggest decision ever. When I returned to the kitchen, I handed the music box to Thabisa.

"This is yours now," I said. My eyes watered, even

though I was smiling.

Thabisa shook her head. "What do you mean?"

"I want you to have it. You're my best friend, Thabisa."

"I can't—"

"Please." I sniffled as I placed the music box in Thabisa's hands. "It's a token of friendship."

Thabisa opened the music box and "Forever Your Friend" played. "Thank you. You're so kind."

I felt I could move on with my life without worrying about what others thought of me. I couldn't wait to find out what kind of adventures I'd have with Thabisa and our classmates in Matopos.

About the Author

BEKEZELA BROSCIUS grew up in Zimbabwe. She holds an M.F.A. in Writing for Children and Young Adults from Hamline University and she lives in Pennsylvania with her husband and son.

www.bekezelabroscius.com

Made in the USA
Lexington, KY
08 October 2018